THE WOMAN WHO FELT INVISIBLE

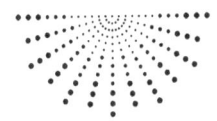

LIZZIE CHANTREE

Lemon Meringue PUBLISHING

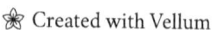 Created with Vellum

With big thanks to Fiona Jenkins and Sue Baker, for being such fabulous supporters of my writing and for all that you do for authors and the book community.

Thank you also, Cora Ryan, for introducing me to a whole group of delightful new book lovers. Big hugs sent to my incredible readers, including the amazing book bloggers who tirelessly share news of my books and make beautiful posts about them. I appreciate you for picking up my novels, telling your friends and family about them and for posting reviews to let other book lovers know about my work. You are superstars!

To everyone in my book group, Lizzie's Book Group. Thank you for taking part in the daily chat, sharing ideas with other members of the group and for creating such a welcoming community of readers and writers.

CHAPTER ONE

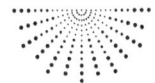

*T*his was it. This was Olivia Tenby's life, now. This was how low she had come. At the age of forty-one, she was sweating her guts out in a house that felt like a furnace, babysitting two delinquent Labradoodle dogs called Bertie and Belle, while their owners swanned around getting even richer somewhere else. Wiping her palms across her face, feeling glad she'd discarded her top so that she couldn't drip on it, she pressed a button. Music blared out of speakers set into the ceiling. This house had everything – lights that came on when you spoke to them, a vacuum cleaner that tripped you over while it scurried along the floor of its own accord, and a fridge that dispensed perfectly shaped ice cubes into crystal glasses.

Olivia looked around furtively for a moment, and then laughed and decided to go for it. Her job as dog sitter extraordinaire had begun two weeks ago. She'd been told to entertain the excitable animals in any way she could think of, as they were naughty and destroyed everything while the owners were out – which they always were. Olivia hadn't even met them, which was baffling. They left her notes with instructions on how to stop the dogs eating the walls and making a mess of the thick pile carpets. She actually quite liked the job, it was as easy as walking in a straight line. Then she thought about how wobbly she always was after three vodka and cokes, and quickly pushed that picture aside. The dogs were bored and, although her job included giving the house a cursory swipe with a duster, it was always immaculate when she arrived. Something was a bit weird, though, as the place was incredibly hot. The dogs liked to slobber all over her, making her even hotter. So she'd taken to stripping off as soon as she sat down with the pooches, otherwise she'd probably pass out and be found weeks later, mummified in dog hair.

She also drank gallons of water, which made her need to pee every five minutes, and the dogs' claws raked her skin whenever she moved, as they jumped up and thought she was about to play. To be fair, there was a lot of skin to scrape. She knew she needed to be fitter, but she wasn't allowed to open the doors and windows and go outside for more than ten minutes. She could shut the dogs in the garden, but that was the only time she could clean. There wasn't much to do but the house was massive and she had to rush round before the dogs barked and wanted to come in again. The poor loves were desperate for company. There was air conditioning in the kitchen for the dogs, and their hair was kept short, but as soon as you opened another door you were hit with a heatwave. Perhaps the owners came from a tropical country and felt cold along the Devonshire coast? She hoped she might meet them one day to ask them.

She'd have to be properly dressed if she did, though. She sighed, looked down at her figure. She liked her curves, even though her old school 'friends' had suggested she shouldn't. A few gorgeously curvy girls were making headlines these days but she bet they didn't eat a slice of cake more than once a week, and cake was one of Olivia's greatest passions. She also enjoyed celebrity gossip magazines far too much. She was her own worst enemy, but who else did she have to admire, if not the stunning men in those magazines? To her, a man who looked as though he enjoyed his food was incredibly sexy. Nothing got her pulse racing more than a date that included a big sausage. Not that she'd had a proper date in years. She'd spent all of her time caring for, or worrying about her dad and his deteriorating health.

She caught her breath for a moment and then listened to the beat, jiggling her chest, making the dogs jump around her legs. She grinned at them and wiggled her hips in time with the music. She grabbed two curtain tie-backs that had tassels on the end and swung them in circles from her chest, giggling. She spun around and around until she fell onto the couch in an exhausted heap. The dogs launched themselves at her and she oofed and pushed them onto the floor, dropping the curtain ties and enjoying seeing the dogs gaze adoringly at her, as if she was the only person in the world who mattered.

They had become her best friends in the last fortnight and she hated having to go home and leave them here. Not that they would fit into her tiny abode, or that she could afford to provide the kilos of food they guzzled in seconds, smiling at her afterwards with stinky, whiskery faces. At least they appreciated her sense of humour. She didn't have anyone else to try her jokes out on. She winced and pulled up her tight jeans. They were probably a size too small, but she hadn't been paid for this work yet and had no money to shop. Her other job, as stationery supervisor for a big information technology firm, didn't exactly set the world alight and fill her bank account either. She grinned when she thought of her sexy boss with his big blue eyes and swishy blond hair. He was a real dreamboat. He made her body blush from head to toe and her heart beat faster. She sucked her stomach in and vowed to make a change and buy clothes that fitted her, instead of ones she wished did.

She liked her job, but as her hours changed each week, she hadn't really made friends or become part of the work group. She could sometimes go a whole day without talking to another human being at her dog sitting job and in the office, everyone ignored her. Being over forty didn't help. She felt like an invisible woman. People walked past and bumped into her without realising she was there and, although she had previously had rampant sex quite regularly, it was always furtive and quite often in a car, which was uncomfortable and slightly mortifying. Now she'd moved to a new role, the sex had stopped and she'd gone back to being invisible again. His hours hadn't worked with hers, even though she'd have happily met him after work every day, or just stayed in his bed until he got home.

She couldn't risk getting fired from either job. She'd had two previous posts in the last four months, and been sacked from both of them. She needed to keep this work if she wanted to be able to pay the rent on her little flat. She'd been there for years and really should have moved on by now, but at forty-one, time was marching by and she couldn't face trying to fit in somewhere new. Mr Benson from next door didn't mind her playing music with the windows open, as he was half deaf and her other neighbours worked during the day and partied all night, so she only met them for a slight nod of the head as they brushed past her on the front step.

Trying to think of a new way to entertain the dogs, she picked up the TV remote from the couch and decided that they could learn to dance while she sang into her improvised microphone. She actually had a decent singing voice and was a master of karaoke at home, and one day she dreamed of having a group of friends to go to a pub with. Perhaps if she did a really good job with the dogs, the owners of this house would introduce her to their own glamorous and exotic circle? After ten minutes of vigorous dancing and rather spectacular singing, the dogs fell into an exhausted heap and she sank down with them onto the floor and rested her head on Bertie's underbelly while Belle watched on. Sighing in bliss, she decided to have a five-minute snooze before the dogs got restless and wanted to play again.

In the corner of the room, a tiny red light flashed on a discreet CCTV camera. It moved slightly to focus on Olivia and the dogs, while they fell into a dreamless sleep.

CHAPTER TWO

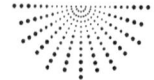

*O*livia pulled at the hem of her fetching cranberry crushed velvet dress and wished her face wasn't the same colour. She hated going to parties alone and glanced around for a friendly face but couldn't find one. Her chest was determined to escape her décolletage and she'd been holding in her stomach for an hour. She stood on her own, watching Alex from accounts and Karen from HR snog in front of everyone and wished she knew the right things to say to make her colleagues want to speak to her. They were on the dance floor of the venue her employers had hired for the annual Christmas party. Everyone was in high spirits – literally. They'd almost drunk the bar dry, and several of them had tried to break into the kitchens to take photos of their backsides on each other's phones or to have furtive sex.

The minimal room décor with slate grey walls and chrome surfaces, was tasteful, but the garish decorations that her boss, Greg, had made them put up earlier, including the wonky Christmas tree that drunken revellers had bumped into at least a thousand times already, made the place look more like a downmarket Santa's grotto. Greg insisted it was kitsch.

Olivia loved it, too. She smiled and then caught sight of her boss. The grin slid from her face. She pressed herself up against the wall to blend in, then realised that no one had even said hello to her yet, even though she'd been there since the start of the evening. She hardly needed to worry about gorgeous Greg walking her way. He had a permanently pained expression on his face these days, whereas he'd always taken the time to acknowledge her before. She felt the loss of this tiny titbit of human contact.

Watching him march up to the bar, Olivia saw a small curvaceous woman trailing behind him, then giving up and going to sit on a tall stool at the other end. Her legs were so short, she had to lift one buttock up first, and then pull the rest of her body after her until she was more or less balanced on the stool, looking like she might topple off at any moment.

Greg laughed uproariously at something his leggy personal assistant, Jen, whispered in his ear. Olivia frowned. She was sure she saw Jen flick her snakelike tongue out and lick his earlobe, but when she blinked they were chatting normally. Olivia shrugged and looked at the forlorn figure on the stool. Perhaps she was Greg's date, and he was bored with her already. It seemed like Jen was flavour of the month. Olivia had even seen Jen sitting on Greg's lap in his office after everyone else had left for the day, when she was trawling around refreshing the stationery.

Bile rose to Olivia's throat. Jen always wore a fake smile and looked down her nose at other women, as if they were competition. Olivia mentally crossed her off of the list she'd drawn up of potential friends at work, not knowing why she'd added Jen in the first place. She barely acknowledged Olivia's existence. Olivia's hips gyrated to the music. She couldn't help it. Her body had a mind of its own when it heard a beat. Dancing was something she was good at. Endless hours of modern, ballet and tap lessons had been foisted on her as a child, even though she'd almost died of shame each time her mum had tried to squeeze her into that bloody pink tutu – the same one she'd found at the back of her wardrobe in a cardboard box, and had fun putting on the dogs last week. They'd looked adorable, while she'd felt ridiculous, even when she'd been young.

She tried to control her body and keep it in check. Everyone would laugh at her if she hit the dance floor. She couldn't do her best sexy moves without rubbing her body against someone, and they'd probably have her arrested! She longed for a delicious dance partner. She looked at Greg and then at Alex from accounts and her stomach sank. She could see they liked much younger women, even if they were sharp and scowled like Jen did, whenever she deigned to speak to Olivia.

Olivia realised she'd been so deep in thought that her sparkly Christmas shoes had shimmied her straight across the dance floor and over to the far end of the bar without her even noticing. The petite woman looked at her sympathetically and pulled out another bar stool for her, which Olivia lifted her bum onto gratefully.

'Happy Christmas,' said Olivia lamely. The woman grinned at her, which made her face light up. Olivia felt like she was bathed in sunshine.

'Happy Christmas. Are you here with someone?' the woman asked.

Olivia's heart always stopped for a second when anyone asked her this question. She wished for once she could gaze across a crowded room and single out a hot hunk who was already staring her way proprietorially. It hadn't happened yet. She still had time, a spark of hope said, before she snuffed it out.

'No, I'm just the office stationery supervisor,' said Olivia. 'You?'

'I'm Greg's wife.' Olivia had just taken a big swig of her drink and almost spat it out. She gulped it down instead and started coughing, feeling the alcohol burning her throat. The woman slapped her on the back, concern in her eyes. 'Are you ok?'

Visions of Jen straddling Greg's lap at work filled Olivia's mind and she tried to stop her face from flaming. She hated being in on a secret, as she usually blurted it out by mistake. The saying about shoot the messenger was so true, in her experience anyway. In her old job she'd been able to find out anything about anyone, but she'd left that past behind her and she wasn't going back. She managed to take another small sip of wine into her constricted throat.

'I'm fine…' she spluttered, breathing in and really looking at the woman before her for the first time. Her clothes were expensive and immaculate, she didn't have a blonde hair out of place. 'Uh… how lovely. Have you been married for long?'

Olivia was glancing around and was primed and ready to run to the nearest exit. The boss's wife would no way want to be trapped talking to her. They must have been married for like – a minute.

'Almost twenty-five years.'

Olivia's eyes bugged out and she gripped the sides of the stool. 'Did you meet at playschool?' The woman's face was unlined and she didn't look a day over thirty.

She laughed at that though, and patted Olivia's arm happily.

'That's so funny! I'm forty-eight. We married when we were both twenty-three. He was working as an apprentice for my dad and we fell in love.'

Olivia realised that her mouth was hanging open unattractively and snapped it shut. Love... bloody hell.

'I thought Greg was in his late thirties, but you look amazing. Maybe thirty-five,' said Olivia honestly, not mentioning she was terrible at assessing people. She had stopped doing it after offending her first boss, asking when the baby was due and getting sacked because the woman was not expecting a child. She'd owned a sweet shop and scoffed half her stock, so it was hardly surprising, but Olivia had spent her days measuring out sweets for other people and had never dared touch the confectionery in case it brought on the wrath of her boss. The woman hadn't been able to look at her without spitting after that and the redundancy notice hadn't been a surprise, if she was brutally honest. She had stuffed her pockets with sweets on her way out and then almost made herself sick sitting behind a tree in the local park, eating every single one of them. The thought of liquorice still turned her stomach to this day.

'I was pretty worried about coming here tonight. I'm Constance, but my friends call me Connie,' said the woman, holding out a hand. Olivia stared at it for a fraction too long before leaning forward to grasp her cool palm.

'Why would you be worried? You're the boss's wife.'

The words still felt strange in her mouth. Olivia tried to smile, but her face was set in a manic grin that would scare children. Greg was a complete charlatan. This woman seemed so sweet and kind.

'Greg always leaves me on my own. He wants me to mingle, but hates me even within touching distance of another man. So I pretty much stay on my own. The girls can be... cliquey.'

Olivia felt the false smile drop and a real one unfurl. Finally, someone else who understood how mean some of the other women in the office were. There were a few nice ones, but even they didn't try and chat to her very often. 'I'm happy to sit with you, if you'd like company? I know he said he doesn't like you talking to men, and I do have a bit of a moustache, but the bleach didn't work and I ran out of time to get a new kit,' she winked.

Connie frowned, then burst into laughter, reaching towards Olivia and briefly touching her leg. 'You are so funny!' Connie's whole face lit up when she smiled and Olivia could see what Greg had been attracted to, other than the obvious curvaceous body and perfect teeth combo. Olivia looked down at her own figure and took a tiny breath in to try and make more room in her dress, but just succeeded in pushing her chest out further. She was sure her dress had shrunk in the wash.

Olivia saw Greg look towards her and Connie and frown, but Jen giggled and caught his attention again. It made Olivia all the more determined that his wife would have a good time.

'Did you know that I have an incredible skill to match people's personalities in the office to pens?' Olivia could have slapped her own face for trying to think up inane chat, but it was too late now and she hadn't been able to think of anything else in her wine fugled brain. She was still shocked that Greg was married.

Connie laughed. 'No. Really?'

'Yep. For Greg, it's a serious and streamlined pen,' she omitted to add *deadly boring but sexy*. 'For Alex in accounts, it's a pen that you can rub out, as he's always saying the wrong thing at the most inappropriate moments and Allie on reception threatens to report him at least once a week.'

As Connie giggled, Olivia's eyes narrowed in on Jen and her indecently short dress, her talons just resting on Greg's arm. 'For Jennifer, the new personal assistant, it's a bright gold sparkly pen. She insists on it and it fits her perfectly –

she's prickly and sharp. Until you get to know her of course...' Olivia laughed with false gaiety.

Connie looked over at her husband and the hot pink nails that were resting on his arm and took a big gulp of wine. Olivia followed suit. They both turned to watch the dance-floor instead. Two men were trying to outdo each other by bumping chests. 'What type of pens do you give them?'

Olivia grinned. 'They have standard writing pens, as they come in packs. You never see one without the other. I think they must hold each other's willies when they pee, they are literally joined at the hip.'

Connie almost spluttered out her drink and now it was Olivia's turn to pat her on the back. 'Sorry, did I say that out loud? I've had a glass of wine too many and my mouth's running away with me. I really should go home,' she said, wobbling slightly as her face grew hot.

Connie wiped her mouth with a napkin but her eyes were twinkling. 'This is the most fun I've ever had at a Christmas party. Let's grab a bottle of wine and hide in the corner getting drunk. You can tell me all the secrets you find out hiding in the stationery cupboard.'

Olivia giggled. This could be interesting. The part of her brain that told her she shouldn't share secrets with the boss's wife had long gone to sleep and it made her skin feel warm and tingly to finally have someone of her own to talk to at the party. She wasn't a wallflower sipping a drink on her own, she was an important person who was entertaining the boss's wife – while the boss himself had his ear licked by a member of staff, and even stuck his hand up her skirt when he thought no one could see him.

Smiling brightly at her new friend and spotting a secluded table, Olivia grabbed her hand and the wine that was on the bar and made a beeline for the start of a new and exciting life.

CHAPTER THREE

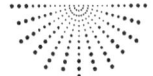

$\mathcal{I}$n the cold light of day, at work the next morning, Olivia wondered if her evening with Connie had been a dream. She recalled lots of cackling laughter and worried about what she'd said. She really couldn't remember much. Connie had kept the wine flowing but refused Olivia's offer to contribute, which was good because her bank account was painfully empty at the moment. She kept getting flashbacks of what she'd said and cringing. She hoped she hadn't blabbed too many secrets about the staff. They didn't notice she was there half the time, and they back stabbed each other and admitted pinching stationery to use at home without worrying that she'd tell on them. They just didn't care. It would be their word against hers, after all, and who would believe someone who worked in a cupboard? If only they knew… she stopped that train of thought before it got her into trouble and she avoided looking at the beautiful new computers that had been set up for some of the staff the night before the party. Her fingers itched to try them, but they weren't hers to play with.

Noticing movement out of the corner of her eye, she

wrinkled her nose as Greg walked towards her, as annoyingly sexy as ever. For once he didn't avoid her and was looking straight at her. She tried to back into the cupboard, but he followed her in. The air immediately seemed to have been sucked out of the place.

'Can I help you, Greg?' she asked, turning and picking up some pens, hoping he wouldn't notice the bags under her eyes and her post-party, alcohol breath.

Greg looked her up and down, making her squirm. 'You look nice today. Thank you for entertaining my wife at the party. That was above and beyond the call of duty. What on earth could you have found to talk about, though?' he asked, his voice saccharine-sweet. She cringed and made a sick face as he glanced around the cupboard as if he'd never seen it before – which he probably hadn't. Who wanted to be bothered by a tiny box filled to the brim with pens and paper? He moved a little too close for comfort as he turned back. His chest was almost touching hers, making her jab the pen she was holding into his hand by mistake.

'Ouch!'

'Oh sorry, Greg,' she gasped, trying not to smirk. She winced afterwards as she pictured him sacking her for stabbing him. That wouldn't go down well on her curriculum vitae. He looked furious.

Greg put his hand to his mouth to try and ease the pain. She could tell he had a burning issue to discuss with her. Just as he was about to say something, though, a group of staff walked past and glanced their way. He huffed and headed back towards his office.

She shook slightly, but seeing a few other staff members in the little kitchenette at the back of the office, she took a deep breath and went to join them. She smiled at one woman and tried to chat, but was ignored. One fairly young girl with a long brown hair looked at her with pity and offered her a coffee, but as the others glanced their way and filed out, she shrugged by way of apology and rushed after them, leaving Olivia feeling stupid and not knowing what to do. The coffee jar was now empty and even the tea bags looked like they'd seen better days. The person who looked after supplies for the kitchen needed to do a better job, or Olivia was coming for them.

Then she remembered what it was like to have a 'friend,' and stormed back to her pen cupboard. It was time that Connie found a better man than Greg, and knew what a toad her husband was. Without thinking, she picked up one of the sparkly gold pens that she had told Connie about and hid it up her sleeve. Feeling her heartbeat ramp up, and wishing her head wasn't still pounding so much she couldn't think clearly, she sidled along the wall to Greg's office, like a spy in an old movie. Noticing that he was talking to the sales team in another office, she took a huge lungful of air and felt the weight of the pen as if it was an iron bar.

She tiptoed into the office, located Greg's briefcase and slipped the pen inside, positioning it right at the bottom. Hearing voices outside she stood up and refilled the pens in the pot on the desk from a stash in her trouser pocket, before rushing back to the cupboard. No one had glanced her way, but she was out of breath and her palms were sweating. Breathing deeply and leaning against the wall of the stationery cupboard, her head spun as if she'd just run a marathon, but she was also a bit elated. One tiny victory.

It was possible that Greg might find the pen himself and throw it away, but she hoped he didn't clear out his briefcase that often. Olivia pictured her own handbag, which was full of sweets, money which probably wasn't even legal tender anymore and old dog chews, and cringed inwardly.

Greg would be horrified to know Olivia had swapped phone numbers with Connie. He'd hate to think of his wife being friendly with the staff, but Olivia was beyond caring. Connie had made time for her and she was returning the favour. Stupid to think it would work, or that Connie would even understand the significance of the sparkly pen if she did check her husband's briefcase. She might not suspect that he was a cheating scumbag.

Olivia felt proud she had solved an issue without resorting to her old tactics, then seconds later regretted acting on her hungover instincts, but it was too late now. Greg walked back into his office with a woman from accounts and shut the door behind them. Sticking her tongue out at the closed office, Olivia instantly forgot about Greg as she noticed it was almost midday. She was supposed to be letting the dogs out and cleaning today. She hoped the owner didn't have another indoor assault course set up for the dogs, like last week. Belle and Bertie had refused to do any of it and she had ended up having to hop between the jumps and hoops to get them to even try. In the end, they just chewed them up and then spat them out in disgust. For some reason, her dancing immediately mesmerised them, so she tended to do that now, although she always covered up these days, so they couldn't scratch her skin. She could let loose and at least the dogs wouldn't laugh at her. She was also getting a bit fitter, but in a fun way. Who needed spin classes when you had dog agility?

CHAPTER FOUR

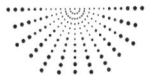

*G*abe Henson lifted the binoculars and focused them in on Olivia's backside as she entered the house. He couldn't help it. She had a sizeable derriere and it jiggled as she walked. He blinked and tried to see beyond her and into the house, cursing as he'd missed his tiny opportunity while ogling. He'd been tracking her for weeks now and he was confused as hell. He'd been given this job by his superior at the police station and he wasn't happy about it. Gabe was a detective and this sort of work wasn't in his job description. It wouldn't usually fall to a senior officer to do a stakeout like this. He really had irritated his boss and he was making a statement by sending Gabe there. He tried to refocus his mind. Since he'd first set eyes on Olivia and seen the videos she posted online, he couldn't work her out.

She owned the house, but didn't live in it. From the videos online, she was an influencer who was famous for her dancing dog clips. She'd already got quite a following for the first one, dancing in her bra. It had over a million hits. She'd cleverly blurred her face out, which must have taken hours of work as she moved around a lot! Perhaps her video career funded this humongous house, but probably not. If he was right, then the tipoff that she was growing a whole crop of cannabis on the third floor meant she could afford to put her feet up and mess around with the dogs. It was pretty risky on her part, though, or over-confident.

He'd done some background checks and the electricity costs for her house were through the roof. It must be like a furnace inside. No wonder Olivia liked walking around in her underwear. She was taking such a chance, putting herself on social media. Yet he could see why she did it. Dog clips were popular and this woman had serious, jaw dropping curves, though you'd never guess from the ill-fitting jeans and baggy T-shirts she always wore outside. They literally hung straight down from her breasts, and added pounds to her middle. Not that he'd been studying her figure... it had been research.

She had another tiny flat and slept there at night. But why she would pick something so small, when she could live full-time in the whitewashed monstrosity in front of him, he couldn't work out. The house looked like a castle, and was exactly that, keeping everyone else out. Perhaps her dealer lived in the flat, and she slept with him there each night? The thought didn't quite sit well with him, for some reason.

It didn't add up, and he hated loose ends. He knew some criminals liked to pretend to be poor but had a king's ransom stuffed under the floorboards. But then, why have an ostentatious house like this, and visit it every day?

He was under pressure from the higher echelons at the police station to work this one out, but unless they had a good reason to enter the house, he had to keep his distance. He was tempted to ask his contact to hack the video feed Olivia used for her videos. But his bosses were watching him and he had to do things by the book this time, however much it irritated the hell out of him.

He took a sip of his cold coffee. He threw it onto the passenger seat in disgust, before realising there had still been some liquid left in the cup. It went everywhere. Swearing, he grabbed a napkin and mopped up, shoving the whole soggy mess into the glove compartment.

CHAPTER FIVE

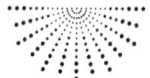

*C*onnie's hand touched something prickly in Greg's briefcase. She frowned and opened the bag to get a better look at what it was. The bright gold sparkly pen was like a beacon at the bottom. She picked it up between two fingers as if it was poisonous and dropped it on the bedside table. The shower was still running, so she knew she had a moment to catch her breath before Greg came out. This was a sign.

She recalled the woman she'd met at the works Christmas party. Olivia, that had been her name. She'd thought of her a few times since then. She'd seemed as lonely as Connie herself was. Olivia had given Connie her number at the end of the evening, and Greg had noticed. He hadn't been happy about it. He'd even mentioned Olivia on the drive home, saying she was creepy and always watching him. Connie had thought she was hilarious, but no one else appeared to give the woman the time of day. They all had their own little gangs and it seemed Olivia was like a square peg in a round hole. She didn't fit in, or conform for some reason. Connie was sure Olivia saw more of Greg at work than Connie did at home though. The house seemed eerily quiet these days.

Connie pictured Jen the secretary, in that tiny pink dress. She remembered the way the girl had whispered into Greg's ear and then thrown her head back and laughed, making her silky blond mane of hair swoosh around her slim neck. Instead of feeling sick, as she had the first time she'd suspected Greg of cheating, now she had proof... almost. She'd been unsure for years, thinking Greg might be unfaithful, but he worked long hours, running her dad's company. And he had always been too clever to be caught. Whichever way she looked, he'd been clean. When she'd asked him, he'd denied it and she'd had nothing concrete – until now.

But Olivia was trying to help her, she could tell.

She scrabbled around in the drawer of her bedside table for the paper with Olivia's phone number. Finding it, she quickly tapped out a text asking Olivia to meet at a coffee shop the next day. Then she shoved the phone, the number and the offending sparkly gold pen back in the drawer, just in time. The shower shut off and the bathroom door opened. She looked down to see her hand was trembling.

Her stomach ached and she rubbed it gently, then she pressed her nails into her palm and wondered if he was cleaning another woman from his skin. She winced. He must be exhausted from so many extra 'creative' meetings.

It was her family business he was running into the ground while he wasn't concentrating on work. If it wasn't for her ideas for developing new software to sell, the company would have gone under years ago. She was fed up with Greg taking credit for her work. She wanted him gone. Greg had even convinced her dad that the ideas were his. It was becoming tiresome.

He had stopped paying her any attention recently and she was sure it was down to his assistant, whom Connie now hated with a passion. She wished she could find a way to get her sacked. Olivia was her only hope of that. Perhaps he really liked this one?

The problem was that, although she'd asked him to sign a prenuptial agreement, it had been very basic... for goodness sake, she'd been in love! She was such an idiot. The contract didn't say anything about the company, as it had been fairly new when they'd met. She had wondered from time to time if Greg had married her quickly when he'd realised how well the company might do. But then he would sweep her up and kiss her until she couldn't think straight and she completely lost her mind.

There was a clause in the paperwork about being unfaithful, but to date he'd made her feel as though she was paranoid. She had thought for a time that she was going mad. When he'd dragged her along to the Christmas party this year, she'd even considered medication to get herself through it. Now she was in focus and saw everything clearly. Olivia had helped with that and Connie would be eternally grateful. Connie didn't think Olivia was weird, just a bit of a misfit who longed to slot in beside everyone else.

Hearing the ding of the reply on her phone made her wince. She hoped Greg wouldn't notice. But he was too busy preening in front of the mirror like the peacock he was. Her stomach sank heavily, filled with loathing. She didn't pick the phone up, although she was sorely tempted. She needed to get to sleep and plan painful and humiliating revenge on the man who had tried, for years, to ruin her life.

CHAPTER SIX

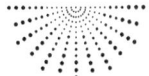

*O*livia sent a reply to the text, then sat in stunned silence, re-reading the message. Greg's wife had invited her for coffee. Had she seen the pen? Did she know what it meant? Olivia wondered if she was about to lose yet another job. She'd checked the company out online the night before and discovered that Greg and Connie were both directors. Online articles suggested that Greg would be running the whole thing when Connie's parents retired. What a nightmare.

Olivia had responded to that text with a yes, of course. She would have to reschedule her dog sitting, but who could say no to the boss's wife? Even if it meant Greg might give her the sack. Now she wished she hadn't scoffed a whole bar of chocolate, after dunking it into milky coffee with extra caramel syrup, until it had melted into a delicious, lumpy mess. Why the hell had she put that garish sparkly gold pen in his briefcase? She chastised herself. It had been stupid. She vowed never to drink so much again, and not to have bright ideas when she had a hangover.

She got up to make herself toast. It would soak up some of the coffee and chocolate. She added a big dollop of jam for good measure, but couldn't be bothered to scrape the last of it out of the jar. Life was a currently a learning curve. She had once tried adding a little bit of water to the jar and giving it all a good shake, but the resulting red sludge had made the bread soggy and it had dropped into her lap on the way to her mouth. She still hadn't managed to get the mark out of her beige trousers. A huge stain on your crotch was never a good look for anyone – but then neither were beige trousers.

Munching on her toast, she mentally ran through her wardrobe and wondered what to wear, wishing she hadn't donated most of her clothes to charity when she couldn't squeeze into one fitted top and she'd been miserable about her dad passing away. The last time Connie had seen Olivia, she'd been looking classy and exotic, wearing her crushed velvet dress. But the rest of her clothes were now jeans and T-shirts, or black trousers and the two baggy white blouses she wore for work. She recalled her old look, but then pushed that thought aside. She had given away every single half-fashionable item she'd owned. The only things she'd hung onto were her trusty cranberry number and the black sexy dress that her best friend, Darius, had bought her. It was screwed up at the bottom of her wardrobe somewhere.

She preferred her more comfortable clothes now. Who needed silk when you had Lycra? Then she grinned and remembered a top she had won by taking part in an Internet competition. She had to stop herself from entering loads of them when she was bored. She could so easily have become addicted to all the bounty you could win, but she didn't have space to store anything in her flat and she certainly didn't want to attract the attention of the police by winning too many prizes. Those competitions were sometimes easy to fix when you knew how.

She had only entered this particular contest because she had to describe her dream date, and she'd got a bit carried away. When the prize arrived it been a stretchy branded top, a mini-bottle of wine and some chocolates with a fancy name she'd never heard of. She ate them, but only because she felt bad about not appreciating the prize. The top was still in its bag and the wine had disappointingly only lasted about two gulps.

Dropping her burnt toast crusts in the sink, and wishing the air didn't smell as though she'd set fire to the flat, she ran into her room, which only took two steps as it was next door. She rummaged around at the bottom of the Formica wardrobe her uncle had given her, and then sat back on her haunches in glee. The top was a stretchy size large in a soft blue colour. Ok, it did have the company slogan over the left breast, but as Constance was unlikely to have heard of it, Olivia could pretend it was a bit posh, like Gucci.

Throwing the packaging on the floor and pulling on the top, she turned this way and that and decided the new look worked. She usually wore stretchy tops under a big white T-shirt, but today she actually felt a bit sexy. Bit much for coffee? Nah.

She went and stuck her head upside down under the bath taps and turned the water on. She grimaced as it was freezing cold at first, but she rubbed in some foamy and fragrant shampoo and quickly washed and then dried her dark hair, leaving it disappointingly looking exactly the same as it had fifteen minutes before. She stuck her tongue out at her reflection and grabbed her handbag. Wondering briefly if she had time to empty out the half-eaten bags of sweets, emergency teabags and make-up that had probably passed its sell-by date, she wrinkled her nose and decided that could be a job for another night. For now, the extra weight would be toning her arms as she walked, which meant she was multi-tasking. Why bother trekking to the gym when you had a heavy handbag? She took one last look around her half-messy, half-clean flat and closed the door behind her.

CHAPTER SEVEN

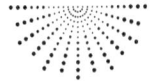

*C*onnie waited. She tapped her perfectly painted nails on the table top in the café where she had chosen to meet Olivia. She knew it meant that Olivia would have to travel, but Connie was in the middle of a project and was determined to make a name for herself this time. She would go straight to her father and not show Greg. She couldn't wait to see the surprise on her Dad's face – and the horror on Greg's.

Olivia burst into the restaurant in a top the colour of the sea, that washed out her pale skin. Connie really would have to take that girl in hand, she decided. She didn't know why she thought of Olivia as a child, she remembered she was over forty, but she really did behave like an adolescent. Connie kind of liked it, though. It made a change from the crowd she usually had to hang around with. Mostly they were the children of her parents' friends. Many were retired now, and deadly boring. All they ever talked about was the size of their estates, or their wallets. Connie wondered if she was boring too. Was that why Greg strayed? Olivia could possibly help with that too. They could help each other.

Waving to catch Olivia's attention, she smiled and watched her shimmy her way between the tables. Connie had seen her sashay across the dancefloor at the Christmas party, and the girl had moves.

Connie had already ordered two cappuccinos and two Danish pastries and Olivia's eyes lit up when she saw them. She obviously wasn't a woman who held herself back in company. She had soft curves and a nice face with a few freckles dotted over her nose, and seemed at home in her own skin. The tight top accentuated her breasts and Connie didn't know where to look.

Olivia bent down and awkwardly kissed Connie's cheeks, hovering as if waiting to be invited to sit. This wasn't a job interview! Connie inclined her head towards the chair and Olivia sank into it gratefully and wrapped her hands around the coffee. It was cold outside and she must be freezing. Connie didn't see a coat, just a jumper thrown over her arm. Olivia's nose was a bit red, but then so was the rest of her face. She was pretty, but she definitely didn't make the most of it. Someone else with those black lashes would cover them in stroke after stroke of mascara, to make her big brown eyes pop. She should also wear stronger colours and have her hair highlighted and cut. It was ok, but a bit muddy in shade, and messy.

Olivia certainly knew how to draw attention to her curves, though, as the man on the next table was practically drooling into his coffee at the logo across her breast. It was stretched to twice its normal size and was the shape of a circle, like a target on a darts board, which was unfortunate as it looked like a huge nipple. Connie gave the man a death stare until he flushed and looked at his lap, then seemed to decide that wasn't the best idea either and shoved the news-paper he'd been reading onto his legs, before grabbing his cup and drinking his tea, eyes firmly fixed on a speck of chipped paint on the wall.

Connie wished she had the confidence to wear more fitted clothes, but Greg often commented that they didn't suit her. She knew she could do with losing a few pounds, but she ate when she was nervous or cross – and Greg made her both of those, every day. She vowed to stop being such a wet blanket, to take back the control that Greg had syphoned from her and from the business. She should have taken over herself by now, and she would have, had she not married such a controlling man.

For some reason, Connie felt that Olivia was the key to her happiness. Since meeting her, she felt empowered and fierce. The more she saw Olivia, the more it seemed that she didn't care what people thought of her. She was who she was, without trying to be someone else. It was a breath of fresh air and Connie intended to learn from her, even if it meant having a new friend who was slightly messy and uncouth.

'Sooo… you wanted to see me?'

Connie stirred her coffee and took a moment to inhale the aroma and wait for the blood to stop rushing around her veins. 'I got your message.'

Olivia's skin flushed an even darker shade of red and she gulped down some of the still-scalding coffee, before placing her cup back on the saucer and raising watery eyes to Connie and fanning her mouth with her hand. 'About that… I'm sorry. I don't know what I was thinking. I might have been the tiniest bit hungover from the Christmas party. You did order two extra bottles of wine.'

Connie's eyes narrowed. 'So you made it up?' She held her breath, waiting for the answer. Perhaps she was imagining things, and Greg wasn't a philandering scumbag after all.

Olivia started shredding the edge of her paper napkin until a little hill of red mess was piled in front of her. Connie waited patiently but her heart was thudding in her chest. 'Ah… no. Well – not exactly.'

The air whooshed out of Connie's lungs and she grabbed onto the sides of the table to try and stop herself from shouting and stamping her feet, or passing out. Either her husband was sleeping around, or she needed to work out why she felt a burning urgency to check his phone and wallet every day. Greg was making her feel like she didn't know her own mind, and she was starting to worry that he might be right. He was the love of her life, but such a disappointment. One moment he couldn't get enough of her curves and prowess in the bedroom, the next he could barely look at her. She knew she was an attentive lover, so why did he make her feel like such a loser? For some reason, she sensed the woman before her could answer these questions.

'So it's true?'

Olivia bit her lip and then held the coffee cup up in front of her face, as if that would shield her from what was coming next. Her eyes peeped over the rim and she looked tired. For the first time Connie saw sadness and worry lines, and not Olivia's usual smile. 'It wasn't my place to tell you, and I understand if you've brought me here to fire me.' She put down the cup and scooped the napkin detritus into it, looking at it despondently. 'I bet Greg's fuming. I liked you when we met and didn't want to see him hurting you, but I can see I've hurt you too.'

Connie ground her teeth, brushing away the surprising tears that were seeping from her eyes. She dried her face with her own napkin, wincing as the harsh paper scratched her skin. She'd thought she was prepared to find out the truth, but obviously not.

'I haven't told Greg.'

Olivia's eyes went wide and her mouth formed an O. 'How come?'

'Because he's cheating on me! For years he's made me feel like I'm unhinged when I've asked him if he's being unfaithful. He hides it so well.'

Connie saw Olivia gawp at her honesty. Perhaps she didn't have much experience of having girlfriends to talk to, or confiding in someone. Now she reached over and took Connie's hand. Connie noticed Olivia's was shaking. 'Seriously?' she said. 'I thought this might be a one off. I saw him in his office with Jen, but I haven't noticed him with anyone else.'

Connie looked into Olivia's eyes to see if she was lying, but as Connie was useless at discovering liars, she then sat back and put her hands in her lap, watching Olivia squirm in her seat instead. Tears formed in Olivia's eyes and plopped onto the table. She wiped them away with the back of her hand. Connie's stomach turned over. She hated the pity in Olivia's eyes.

Connie could feel the anger boil her own tears so that they evaporated. She was suddenly simmering with rage, but trying to contain it. She didn't want to scare Olivia away. 'Why are you crying? Do you have a moron for a husband? Are you married?'

Olivia sighed and took a bite of her Danish pastry. 'No, and no, I'm not. Sorry, food always cheers me up. I feel so sad. It looks like it's been a tough few months for both of us. I can relate to you being hurt by Greg. My boyfriend dumped me a short while ago. I thought I loved him. How wrong can a girl be?'

Connie hesitated for a second, then relented. 'I'm sorry… I didn't know that. I've been harping on about Greg and didn't even ask about your own love life. Men can be such… boys,' she sighed and rubbed her tired eyes.

Olivia smiled through her tears and pulled off a corner of pastry, looking down at it. 'It's ok. He caught me at a bad moment in my life. I wouldn't have gone near him otherwise. He's a bit of a wrong'un. Tried pulling me into a lifestyle I really didn't want. One of those lowlife scumbags that you wished you'd never set eyes on.'

'I wish I'd never set eyes on Greg.'

'Really?'

'Yes. He married me for my dad's company.'

Olivia jumped up and stared at her, aghast. 'What? I thought you said you were in love when you met. Or was that the wine talking? Look, I need more coffee for this. Do you want one?'

Connie looked into her now-empty coffee cup and nodded her assent. She watched Olivia weave away through the tables and wondered if she had the courage to do what she knew needed to be done. Could she cope without Greg?

By the time Olivia returned with two steaming coffees and set them on the table, Connie had decided what she wanted to do. 'I want to be more assertive, like you,' she stated.

Olivia looked around to see if she was talking to someone else and said in a puzzled tone, 'I'm not confident. I tend to make things up as I go along, most of the time. At least I do now. I used to be super-organised and have a nice life, but now things are bit messy. Did… did Greg marry you for your dad's money?'

'We met at university. He was funny, I was clever.' Connie thought for a moment. 'I suppose he was clever, too, with the way things turned out. I had a lot of ideas to bring in more business, but my dad is quite intimidating with outdated views and so is my mum, so Greg offered to present the ideas to them. It worked well. They probably wouldn't have listened to me, although to be honest I never really tried. It became a habit that Greg was loath to break. He likes the limelight, and still uses my ideas. It's time to change.'

'Throw him out!' Olivia banged her hands on the table and made Connie and the man on the next table jump. He was staring at the enlarged logo on her T-shirt again.

'I can't dump him without just cause,' Connie explained. 'We have a prenup. It works in his favour as much as mine. The guy who wrote it was a con artist. Funnily enough, Greg recommended the company and I trusted him. There is an infidelity clause, but I've never been able to prove anything. I could shame him with that, if nothing else, and my dad would ruin him. Greg values his standing in the business community above all else. People revere him. When I got your message, it changed everything for me. I want to prove what he's doing, and I want my parents to realise his work is actually mine. He has always had a way of undermining me. Well, that stops today. Will you help me?'

Olivia sipped her coffee, giving herself a froth moustache. Connie tried to overpower her instinct to wipe it from her face. 'Greg scares me a bit, but I hate him now that he's hurt you, so I agree. How can I help you, though? I work in the stationery department. My work desk is in a cupboard.'

'That's the best place for you to be. From what you told me at the party, people pretty much ignore you at work. They won't even make you a cup of tea.' Olivia flinched again. She'd obviously forgotten being so forthcoming after the second bottle of wine at the Christmas party. 'You'll be able to snoop to your heart's content and no one will suspect what we're doing, especially not *Gorgeous Greg*.' Olivia grimaced – it seemed she'd also forgotten she'd told Connie about his nickname too.

Olivia laughed suddenly. 'He's too busy shagging anything that moves to notice a forty-something pen pusher like me.' Connie's face fell, and Olivia gasped and put hand over mouth. 'I'm so sorry! I'm always doing that. It's why I'd be a useless spy. I always wanted to be one at school, but when I hid behind a wall to try and eavesdrop, my stomach stuck out and gave me away. You really should find someone else to help you. Someone with some tact.'

Connie tried to regulate her breathing. She really wanted Olivia to help her and, other than hiring a private detective, which she'd tried once before, she had little choice. The detective had come up with zilch. Plus, she liked Olivia's quirky personality and she seemed really down on her luck. Connie felt a bit more positive, helping her new friend out. This way perhaps something good could come of the whole Greg mess.

She clinked coffee cups with Olivia, almost chipping her new friend's tooth as she'd been about to sip her coffee, then they both burst into giggles. 'I think you're absolutely perfect for the job and of course, I'll pay you for your time.'

Olivia looked like she was about to protest, but Connie shushed her and got up to go and order them both a sandwich to eat while they worked out how to snare Greg with his pants down. Then she could prove he was a lying lothario – and her parents would have to listen to her at last.

CHAPTER EIGHT

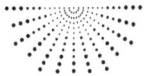

*G*abe stuck his face near his coffee cup and wrinkled his nose. The dregs of his early morning coffee were now acrid and bitter. He wished he had people to make him coffee, like Olivia probably did in that big house. He hadn't seen anyone else go in or out, but he'd only been able to stake it out for a few hours here and there, so far. Perhaps the staff slept in.

He sighed and rubbed his stubbled jaw. He really needed to take better care of himself, but he was going stir crazy with this recently enforced desk job. Ok, he had been shot, but that was months ago and the bullet hadn't hit anything major. It had made him limp for a while, but he was almost mended now. That was if you discounted the agonising pain stopping him sleeping at night every time he lay on his thigh.

His bosses at the police station were worried about anyone finding out that he'd broken protocol by asking a computer 'expert' called Razor to help him out, when the investigation had hit a brick wall. His bosses had raged and called the dude a hacker. Well, he was one, but Gabe thought their reaction was a little extreme. Gabe was hoping Razor could help solve a case that involved a phishing scam. The scammer helped damsels in distress who'd had personal photos stolen and posted online by their ex-partners. He phished the people who had posted them, by tricking them into divulging personal bank details. It seemed like it was a game of payback, but huge sums of money had gone missing. At one point Gabe had thought this particular scammer had retired, but recently he had suddenly become very active again.

Gabe had stumbled across Razor by accident when he had been looking into another case and needed insight from underground contacts in the computer world. They had then tried to track this Damsel case thief together, but the perpetrator had always eluded them at the last minute. He was playing a game with his victims and somehow also knew what the police were doing – but how, Gabe couldn't fathom. Razor had tipped Gabe off that the Damsel scam was a smokescreen for a wider group of criminals who used the same tech. He said they had set the whole scheme up to distract the police from their own criminal activity. Gabe didn't have time to mess about with that. Perhaps it was power play between rival gangs or businesses, but why were so many women involved and pictures stolen and posted online, if it wasn't something personal? It felt like he was stepping into relationship territory, where things had gone sour and someone sought revenge. Perhaps these women were paying a hacker to track down who had posted the photos and make them pay in a different way – where it would hurt most, in their wallets. He hadn't seen money go into any of the victims' accounts, or go out as payment to the Damsel hacker, so everyone was covering their tracks.

His frustration finally dragged him out of the stupor caused by working at a desk all day long. He was sure his legs ached more from siting down doing nothing than from chasing people. His boss was treating him like a school kid and it was starting to grate on his nerves. He even thought he might have developed a scowl, and his mates kept grinning and patting his back when he walked past.

He wouldn't voice it, but he kind of commended what the photo hacker was doing – bleeding dry people who had tried to humiliate their partners in such a distressing way – but his bosses didn't like it and they were getting twitchy. They were also worried about what would happen if the situation escalated.

Gabe wondered what technology Olivia had used in her video to cover her face. It was probably one of those new apps he'd heard about recently. It boggled his mind how quickly different applications were developed. He did speculate, for the first time, if she actually knew that the video had been posted. It was another reason to watch her. Could she be a photo hacker victim, like the other women he'd investigated? But why would she be targeted? Her face was disguised by the app, whereas the other victims could be seen as plain as day. Plus, it was the first use of video he'd discovered. Perhaps the photo shaming had escalated to video shaming? But he couldn't see an obvious connection anywhere and she didn't have a partner who had reported theft of funds. The video she was in was funny and extremely popular, whereas the photos had been humiliating. Mind you, he thought, Olivia might not see the funny side if it had been done without her knowledge, as she was half-naked in it.

He doubted she'd have the know-how to develop software like this. Her job didn't involve computers. She must be earning big bucks from somewhere, though, to afford the house. He remembered the cannabis farm. Perhaps she had lots more houses just like the one he'd seen, unobtrusively tucked away in suburban settings all over the country, and had got bored and decided to become an Internet sensation instead. With a house like that, she could probably afford to pay a specialist to create the video for her. Maybe she'd been hurt by a man, and was making him pay by showing him that millions of others liked watching her? He didn't know enough to be sure of anything, but his brain was whirring with wild assumptions, and his fingers itched to find out.

Gabe had worked out that there was a link between three of the men who had been phished so far. In each case, their funds had been drained. It had been excruciating to get them to talk about what had happened, as all of them were powerful and influential people and were mortified by being duped in a security breech, even though it was a highly sophisticated one. It had been like pulling teeth but he'd managed it at last.

They all had companies in common, so he had requested personnel files from each firm to see if they had any minions working there who might be in on the scam. Someone could have leaked potentially embarrassing information or given access to private documents. It would be unusual for three firms who'd normally be in competition to be acting together, but the payoff would be astronomical if blackmail was involved. It was more likely that the scam was coming from outside with a human mole. He'd seen phishing schemes before and it was a growing problem, so although he was supposed to be keeping an eye on the delectable Olivia and her illegal crop, he was far more interested in the tech problem.

Mindlessly taking a sip of the cold coffee and frowning in disgust, he looked round for someplace to spit it out and then had to hold his nose and swallow. Luckily it was too early for many of his co-workers to be in the office, otherwise they would have had a field day patting him on the back, or sending him animated coffee cups with walking stick memes. He kicked the stupid stick that he was loath to use, but had to rely on occasionally, and grinned when it hit the floor. Some poor bugger could fall over it and break their leg, then perhaps they would stop ribbing him about being a 'hopalong'.

As a man that went to the gym all the time to work off stress, and who was pretty athletic, he hated needing a walking stick. Stuffing two painkillers in his mouth, he remembered just in time not to reach for the blasted coffee cup again and crunched the tablets dry. He tried not to gag and then focused on the documents that he'd already been studying for hours on the computer screen.

Picking up the list of workers, he cursed. There was a name he suddenly recognised. Why hadn't he noticed it earlier? He stood up and his chair hit the floor with a resounding bang. His eyes sparkled for the first time in ages and he bent down to type out a new request for files. Kicking the stick under the nearest desk, he stood up straighter and balanced his weight on his good leg, before striding, albeit a little more slowly than normal, back to his car.

CHAPTER NINE

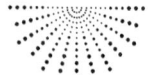

Olivia pulled on her sexy lingerie and then grabbed a plain white T-shirt and flung it over her head. She thought back to the clothes she used to wear, but that part of her was long gone. She didn't want to feel sexy and glamorous any more. She knew her curves attracted men, but they always thought that was the best part of her. They never stayed around long enough to notice that she had a brain. She read in magazines about women being empowered and strong, regardless of their relationship status, but for her it had never quite worked out. She'd simply not had time to take care of her inner-self or give men the adoration and confidence they seemed to desire. She was constantly distracted and had other priorities. She knew she could be doing more with her life, but this was where she chose to be. That's what they couldn't understand. It wasn't for them to understand, though. This was her life. *Maybe that was her strength*, she wondered.

In the end, men demanded more than she was willing to give, except for her last boyfriend. He'd been a shock. She'd started to have feelings for him and he'd shut them down, as if she meant nothing to him. He'd awakened a part of her that she'd thought was long dead. She'd spent so much time alone that she'd forgotten how to interact with people and they had stopped seeing her altogether. She'd been too numb to notice before, but now it made her sad and angry in turn. She didn't deserve to be treated that way by anyone.

Now Olivia finally had time for a man, but she was alone again. Before, boyfriends had been a way to distract herself. The last few years had been hard. But just recently, she'd noticed that she was coming alive again. And meeting Connie reminded her that she wasn't such a lost cause. When Connie said that she admired the way Olivia had behaved, that had meant a lot. Maybe she would now have something to offer a proper relationship, or be stronger on her own. It made her even more determined to help her friend remove Greg's tentacles. He might be gorgeous, but he was a complete jerk.

Connie's wealth meant that she could buy anything her heart desired, even Greg it seemed, but it couldn't stop him from having a wandering eye, or from stealing his wife's brilliant ideas and pretending they were his. What had happened to girl power and sisterhood in this? Who was supporting Connie and helping her to see how amazing she was? Olivia straightened her shoulders and felt that role land squarely on them. She didn't know if she was up to it, but she'd give it a damn good try. If not, she'd ask a few of her old work colleagues from her past life to slip into Greg's inbox and see if there was another way out for her new friend. They had certain skills that went below the radar and although she hadn't spoken to them in years, she knew they were waiting for her if she decided to dip her toe back in. She wasn't sure if she would ever go back there, but it was good to know that they saw something in her and didn't dismiss her as past it, or over the hill.

Looking up as she left the flat, she felt the splash of rain-drops on her face. She really couldn't be bothered to go back inside. She pulled her thin grey coat around her shoulders, shivering as the cold seeped into her bones. The one thing she did still own was her car and she almost sighed with pleasure every time she slid behind the wheel. One of the reasons she stayed in her cramped flat was the parking space right outside her home. Although her car was more func-tional than sporty, it had all the mod cons inside. She'd spent a lot of time driving to and fro from her old job to visit her dad. No matter what was going on in her life, her dad had been her priority. He had been the shining light in her life and the reason she had done everything. A lone tear escaped her eye and she brushed it away before it became a torrent. She pictured his kind face and easy smile and then that image was replaced by someone who was angry and didn't know her name. She sniffed and rubbed her hand across her eyes, trying to erase those memories. She'd always felt safe in her dad's arms and even when he'd got frustrated that he couldn't do so much or remember their past, he still felt like home and she'd abhorred being away from him.

Shrugging off her coat, as she hated driving with anything constricting her movements, she quickly sped into town. It was only about fifteen minutes away. Although it was a hub of industry, the businesses were all a bit boring, like computer conglomerates and data processing agencies. This meant there weren't pretty shops to distract her or deli-cious restaurants to tempt her away from her desk, unlike the smaller town down the street from her flat in the oppo-site direction. Thanks to this, she could get from her front door to her desk in the minimal amount of time. Not that she was a shopper, or had anyone to shop with – except Darius, and his taste was eccentric and beyond her current means. Plus, if she gave him a hint that she was lonely at lunchtimes, he'd camp out at her desk every day and get her fired... again. She had a hunch that he enjoyed seeing her fail. It meant she had more time for him.

Arriving at work, plonking her bottom on her chair and tucking her knees underneath her tiny desk to one side of the stationery cupboard, she tapped her fingers on the surface while she pondered the best way to help her new best friend. Noticing she hadn't painted her nails for a while, she quickly shoved them in her lap as Greg appeared at her shoulder, almost looking down her top, which wasn't even low-cut.

'Hi Olivia,' he said, smiling into her eyes, making her want to vomit in her mouth. She could see how easily women might fall for his charm when it was directed at them. His eyes were the deepest blue and framed with thick luscious lashes. She pressed her nails into her palms to stop herself from being pathetic. This man was a menace, not a sex god.

'Um. Hello Greg. Can I help you?' She stood up so that he had to step back and away from her, but he was still staring rudely at her breasts until she coughed to get his attention.

'Uh... yes.' He grinned as if they had just shared a joke and she frowned. 'I noticed that you were chatting to... my wife... at the Christmas party.'

There was a long pause, and he was suddenly starting to look uncomfortable. 'Your wife's lovely. It was a pleasure talking to her while you were otherwise engaged – with your staff.' She tried to hide her smirk.

Greg frowned and ran his hands through his thick blond hair. She was mesmerised by the movement for a moment. 'Look, Olivia... I want us to be friends,' he said. When he saw the appalled look on her face, he quickly corrected himself. 'I mean,' he cleared his throat. 'All the directors and staff are friendly here, and I've noticed you're on your own a lot. Perhaps you'd like to be moved into the outer office?'

She raised an eyebrow. 'I have plenty of 'friends,' thanks. I'm happy working on my own, but I appreciate the offer, sir.'

Greg flushed. Then Jennifer walked past the cupboard and frowned at seeing Greg and Olivia together, before swishing her hair over her perfectly toned shoulder and waltzing off in a huff at not being able to deliver Greg his usual morning 'ministration'. Olivia wondered if Connie ever checked his collars for lipstick stains. Jen always wore a sharp pink tone that made her lips look enormous.

'I also wanted to say thank you for taking Connie under your wing. She usually hates Christmas parties and it's good to know she has a new girlfriend. I'm sure you understand that you are under a confidentiality contract here, so although Connie's father owns the business, staff still can't mention anything that goes on at work.' Greg's eyes followed Jen, and Olivia had an urge to kick him in the balls.

Greg leaned past her and shut the cupboard door, which forced them chest to chest. Instead of being outraged by her indifference, he seemed to be turned on. 'So you and Connie won't discuss the company or its staff,' he continued.

Olivia was now angry enough to lose another job, over the way Greg treated women. 'Open the door,' she said through gritted teeth. 'We don't discuss you at all!'

His shoulders sagged as he let out the breath he'd been holding. She really wanted to push his pretty face into the plush carpet. He opened the door an inch.

'I care about my staff and just wanted to check that you were ok working in such a confined space,' he said, giving her what he probably thought was a grin so sexy that she would whip off her knickers and mount him for being such an honourable man. It soon slipped when he saw the fire in her eyes.

'I like it in the cupboard.' Olivia replied, imagining slamming his fingers in the door, as she couldn't do it in real life.

'I'll have to come and chat to you more,' he said, sounding like his usual confident self again. She racked her brain for a reason why he would want her attention, other than picturing amazing sex in a cupboard with yet another willing staff member, of course. But he was way off limits, even before Connie became her new best friend. He was her boss.

She took a deep breath, and then said with a sinking stomach, 'I think it's best if I don't see Connie again, full stop. Then you won't worry about any conflict. I don't want to lose this job.'

'You can't do that! She's been happier since she met you, and she hasn't got many friends. I hoped it might make life easier if she had interests other than home.'

Olivia was aghast. Just like that, the anger was back, twice as epic and about to explode. 'So you thought if I kept your wife busy...' Seeing the guilt on his face, she was about to erupt, not giving a toss about the consequences, as the door was pulled fully open. Jen was back, and stood there glaring at them.

'What are you doing in there?'

Olivia looked at Jen with disdain. 'We're plotting how to take over the company so that Greg can kill off his wife.' Jen looked startled for a second and then gave a high-pitched laugh, like a cat being strangled. Greg gave a feeble chuckle too and waltzed off, past Jen, to his office.

'I met Connie last week over coffee,' Olivia smiled sweetly to Jen, her eyes like missiles. 'She was telling me how in love she is with her husband and how they have been happily married for twenty-five years. Isn't that amazing, Jen?'

Jen just stood there, looking like she was sucking lemons, so Olivia looked dreamily around. 'It must be good to still be having sex so often when you've been married that long, mustn't it?'

Jen's eyes were nearly bugging out, as Olivia smiled again and pulled the door shut in Jen's face.

She stood with her back against the shelves, her heart beating like a drum and her chest heaving. She was pretty sure this was what it felt like to step into a boxing ring and psych out your competitor. Not that she was daydreaming about capturing Greg's attention any more. That ship had sailed the moment she'd seen him with Jen, even before she'd found out about his wife. Plus she had rules about dating people she worked with. Never a good idea.

She wasn't into sharing. There were enough men in the world for her to find a single one and, if not, there were always toys. She giggled as she thought of the sex catalogue she'd seen outside her neighbour's flat. The postman had got drenched and half the envelopes were coming apart by the time he'd walked up the path. She had been tempted to swipe the catalogue for herself, but thought poor old Mr Benson probably needed it more than she did… just.

Realising that she would run out of oxygen if she didn't open the cupboard door, she shoved it with her foot and peeked outside. She could see Jen and Greg gesticulating angrily as they paced away along the corridor. Olivia felt a punch of satisfaction. If Greg had been saying he didn't sleep with his wife, then Jen was now a little clearer about the situation she was in. Taking a furtive look around and feeling like a MI5 spy, she sidled along the walls and slipped into Greg's office.

She couldn't pull the blinds down, that would be too obvious, plus she needed to keep an eye out for anyone coming past. Walking to Greg's desk, she tried the drawers. Three opened. After a quick rifle through, she found nothing much, except a half-empty packet of condoms. Yuck. The final drawer was locked. She tugged hard at the handle, but it wouldn't budge.

Thinking fast, she grabbed the briefcase he'd left beside his desk. Bingo! She had noticed that Greg's nails were more manicured than a hand model. Personally, she liked a man with hands that looked like they could show a girl a good time, not one who'd have to ask his valet to do it for him, she sniggered to herself, knowing she was being childish. Wrinkling her nose, she found a monogrammed nail set in the side compartment of the case. She slid it into the lock and tried to wiggle the drawer open with a nail file, like she'd seen in films.

Seconds later, with a resounding snap, the metal file broke in half and almost took her eye out as it flew across the room. 'Crap!' She quickly stuffed the bits into her trouser pocket and hoped she didn't sit on them later and cut an artery.

She'd always known that just because something was expensive, it didn't mean it had any quality or substance, but she'd never had proof until now. She wished she had time to break more of his things, but then he'd definitely know it was her. The problem was that she needed proof that Greg was a cheat to free her friend, without implicating herself. Connie had been completely hoodwinked by Greg, unlike Jen, who knew exactly what she was doing. She deserved all she got.

Taking a deep breath, Olivia touched Greg's computer screen and it sprang to life. The company logo stared at her and she stuck out her tongue at it. It was a shame that Connie's dad didn't recognise what a gem he had in his daughter.

Knowing she really shouldn't be doing this, but unable to stop herself, Olivia used a coder's backdoor to get into the computer and look at Greg's files.

She'd been worn out and broken when she'd arrived here, but she'd always known the temptation of working for a computer company would eventually prove too much. She'd tried to pick the furthest thing from a programmer's job that she could find. For goodness sake, she was in charge of looking after pens and paper, and the computer she'd been assigned to fill in her spreadsheets was antiquated. She'd resisted checking what the old girl could really do as, like her, it was probably assumed to be useless. She'd thought she could ask old friends if she was desperate for help and wouldn't need to go back to her old ways, but here she was, fingers caressing the keys on the keyboard like a lost lover.

She'd been happy with being invisible, until now. She'd only wanted somewhere quiet to lick her wounds. It was just her luck that her new boss, Gorgeous Greg, had a wonderful wife, half-owned the company and wasn't able to keep it in his pants.

Jen walked in just as Olivia was leaving Greg's office, but dismissed her with a flick of her hair. Olivia turned and watched her take a sparkly pen out of her handbag and write Greg a note, probably forgiving him for his bad manners in still making love to his wife. Olivia really needed to go back in and grab that note, but Jen suddenly perked up as Greg sauntered past her, practically shutting the door in her face. It was glass, so the effect was lost as she could still see him, so she gave him a tight smile – and then stuck two fingers up at his back when he walked away. Jen saw, and gave her an evil look. Olivia make a mental note to check the bins for the personal note Jen had just written in case Greg read it and dumped the evidence there, but then glanced at her watch and cursed. She was supposed to have started dog sitting ten minutes ago.

CHAPTER TEN

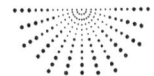

Olivia stomped up the grand stairway to the house and didn't notice the plants had been freshly tended, leaving the fragrance of lavender in the air. She was too cold to care. She'd forgotten to grab a jumper that morning and knew once she got inside the furnace of a house she'd start burning up and sweating, so she hadn't bothered to go back. She opened the door with her key, remembering how the owners had mailed it to her home without meeting her. She'd have to have a word with them about security when they were finally face to face, as it was never a good idea to post your house keys to a complete stranger. She'd given up arriving early or staying late, in the hope of bumping into them, as they seemed to work away a lot. None of the rooms had that much personality, but someone definitely lived there. She could tell from the occasional mess, and the fresh dog food and toys.

The dogs were whiney today, but she still couldn't be cross at them. Who bought two very expensive dogs (she had looked them up and these breeds were a couple of thousand each) and then left them on their own all day? Someone with more money than sense, she decided. The dogs were very high maintenance and wouldn't suit everyone. It was her mission to make them as happy as possible for the few hours she worked every weekday. She even played with all the stupid toys the weird owners left out for her. They must cost a fortune too, but hey, it was their money.

She opened the sliding doors that led from the granite and steel kitchen to the perfectly manicured garden. She frowned as she scanned the garden for the big bins on wheels that most people had. She'd been instructed to leave everything in the garage for the owners to dispose of and wondered once again if they were spies or something, and wanted to check the rubbish to make sure no incriminating evidence was left before incinerating it. She had noticed one of those modern garden furnaces outside last week and it had definitely been used, she could tell by the ash on the ground.

She'd noticed that blue car outside again, parked by the verge next door, when she'd looked for an outside bin earlier, but decided it must be someone visiting another house down the street. It was funny, though, as all the homes had big in-and-out driveways. Maybe the car belonged to a gardener who wasn't allowed to park on the drive. She wondered for a second if she should park her own car in the road and not outside the house, but she shook her head. She was blowed if she was going to do that. She was careful with her car and that was that.

The dogs barked to regain her attention and she slid the doors back for them. They ran around happily, even though their coats were short and it was freezing outside. Picking up some cleaning sprays and cloths stored under the sink, she braced herself and opened the kitchen door, feeling the blast of heat the moment she stepped over the threshold. Wiping her brow, she raced around the ground floor and then had to open a window upstairs. She held her breath for an alarm to sound now that air was in the house, but it didn't happen and she wondered why she hadn't tried that before. The house was so hot it would be back to Mediterranean temperatures in no time, even if she did open a few windows.

Padding upstairs on the soft carpet, she gritted her teeth and pumped her arms, trying to almost propel herself up through the haze of heat. When she got to the top landing, she noticed condensation on the skylight at the top of the stairs. Surely anyone in there would be dehydrated to a prune by now. She had to bring lots of moisturiser when she came, as she worried about her skin ageing twice as fast as normal and her body shrivelling up whilst she worked in this house. She'd end up like an old crone if she wasn't careful. She already felt way past her sell by date, or at least she thought other people assumed she was. They literally looked through her these days. Some even had the cheek to glance around her as if she was in the way. She couldn't remember the last time someone had stared her straight in the eye.

Trying the door, she was tempted to see if they had a nail file downstairs in one of the bathrooms, but after what happened last time she tried to break in at Greg's office, she knew that wasn't much of a burglar. She really, really wanted to know why the door to this floor was always locked, though. It was like someone putting a chocolate in front of you and telling you not to eat it. It was simply ridiculous! She rattled the door knob again and then pushed her weight against it, but it wouldn't budge and it was making her even more sweaty.

She had noticed that the jeans fit her much better lately, so she'd obviously begun to tone up again. She loved her curves, but she had been thinking of ways to curb her recent craving for red wine. She blamed Greg, of course. It was stressful knowing secrets about your boss, and also knowing his beautiful wife. In fact, she would probably blame him for everything for the next two years at least. He deserved it.

She gave the middle floor a quick vacuum and glanced out of the window to make sure that the dogs hadn't turned into mud monsters, as the ground had been a bit wet when she arrived, but they were happily running around in circles chasing each other's tails. She checked her watch and knew she needed to get a move on. The dogs weren't supposed to be out for long, but she was loath to shut them in when they were having fun.

She sprayed and wiped down the shower and then stepped inside to clean that, but leaned on the shower handle by accident. It turned on and soaked her, making her shriek and jump about like a wet dog. Her jeans were soaked through. Argh.

She wondered if the house owners had security cameras outside. Would they see the dogs were still out there and panic? She might lose yet another job. She'd miss the dogs, but not the crazy play the owners expected her to do with them. She was sure they were a bit mentally unstable. She should have checked about surveillance and usually would have, in case she set off an alarm, but she'd been too worn out when she'd begun this job and, to be honest, she hadn't really cared. She tried her best to be a good dog sitter, but she'd never actually owned a dog in her life. She had only answered the ad because it had been on the noticeboard at work. Everyone else had laughed at the stupidity of the tasks, but it had piqued her interest. It had stated that the job applicant would have to entertain the dogs by playing with toys and, as ex-show dogs, they particularly liked dressing up.

She'd applied because she assumed no one else would. She needed a second income, but would have been happy spending her days curled up on a sofa crying and raging at the loss of her dad. She was pretty sure she wouldn't have succumbed to her ex's antics if she'd have been fully compos mentis. She could usually tell a wrong'un a mile off by the way they smelt. She used to have a theory that they gave off a certain hot-man pheromone that made women drool, even when they knew they were bad news. She was distracted, though, and had very little patience with other people since her dad had died.

She put her head in her hands and sobbed for all of the missed years while he'd been unwell and for the amazing dad he'd been all her life, even when he started to forget things and leave the oven on. She'd tried so hard to keep him in the family home and had worked like a demon. It was why she was childless and unmarried, but she wouldn't change a thing, except for the Alzheimer's. It had gradually seeped into her dad's mind and blown his memories into the wind.

As her dad's dementia got worse, it had been too dangerous for him to stay with her. He had required specialist care. She'd hated leaving him at the mercy of the carers at the home he had lived in, even though they were supposed to be the best that money could buy. She'd hacked the surveillance feed for a time to check up on him, but she'd had to stop to protect her own mental health. Seeing him there was so hard. He was being looked after properly and the staff couldn't have been kinder, but she'd needed to feel close to him even when his mind and body were far away.

She'd had to sell the house to pay for doctors' fees, as she'd wanted the best for her dad. She'd been running an IT business from home for some time and it had been very successful. The years she'd spent looking after her dad were useful for distance learning courses and meeting a whole community online. She had only ever met one hacker face to face and she'd grown up with him. Darius was her closest friend. He was a criminal, she knew that, but he loved her and he even sent her homemade jam. That had to count for something. Rubbing her backside on a fluffy towel, she limped gingerly downstairs while her soggy jeans clung to her every move. She slung her damp T-shirt on one of the raging hot radiators by the kitchen door.

Red-faced and almost naked, she was confronted by two very innocent-looking dogs. They had wandered back indoors and had ripped up the bag of toys the house owners had left. It was her own stupid fault for leaving it on the floor. She looked at the remnants to see what had survived. The only things that had been spat out intact were a few juggling balls.

She sighed and tried several times to get them into the air and then grinned at Bonnie and Bertie, who were jumping around her legs. She was actually getting good at this. The balls soared around in the air. The dogs' tongues lolled happily. She wasn't sure what this was doing for them, but they didn't want to go outside again and seemed to enjoy her company, so she launched the balls towards the far end of the huge kitchen and laughed as they slid into each other on the tiled floor to chase after them.

In the corner of the kitchen, a little red light flashed discreetly just beneath the far cupboard by the boiler, which she never used. Olivia waved her hand across a panel on the wall of the kitchen and music blared out of hidden speakers in the ceiling. She started singing at the top of her voice and danced around with the dogs. Her top was finally dry, so she shoved that back on and took a bow. 'The crowd goes wild,' she shouted over the music to the dogs, who looked clueless. 'The imaginary crowd, anyway,' she grinned, flopping down on the couch and immediately being covered with two giant furballs, who tried to lick her neck and covered her T-shirt with dried mud from the garden. She looked down at the designer paw prints and rolled her eyes at Bertie, but he was so handsome that she couldn't be cross with him for long.

She pulled him into her arms and inhaled the scent of puppy dog as she rested her cheek on his back. Once he'd stopped wriggling, it seemed as if he needed that hug as much as she did.

～

*G*abe got an alert on his phone to tell him that another video had been posted and wondered how they did it so quickly. He saw Olivia juggling, heard her actually pretty amazing singing voice and wondered if the people she worked with at the IT company had seen the videos. He supposed it was hard to tell who it was, as her face was covered again, but he could already see the number of views the video was getting. It was another smash hit. He had to laugh at the jumping dogs and exceptionally goofy juggling after what looked like her first few attempts, but the most heart-warming thing was her obvious friendship with the animals. They adored her and he was pretty sure that was the reason why the videos were so popular, along with the fact that she was half-naked again. He tried and failed not to stare while his pulse raced.

The dogs were Internet famous, as was Olivia. They must now have advertisers clamouring to work with them, if they hadn't before. The first video had been posted fairly recently, so maybe it would take time to make money from what she was doing. He wondered if she'd blocked out her face so that her drug-dealing friends didn't find out. Perhaps she was looking for a different career now that her dad had passed away. If he knew anything about criminals, though, they wouldn't let a lucrative contact walk away without a fight.

CHAPTER ELEVEN

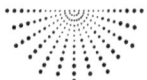

*G*abe watched Olivia shut her front door and wander down the street. The house was in a pretty cul-de-sac but all the facias looked the same. Gabe knew the one Olivia had come out of was divided into three flats. It was happening more and more now as people couldn't afford to live in houses on their own – unless they were Olivia, of course. She had two houses, and one of them was big enough for a whole football team. He checked again and she had only owned the house for a couple of months. Before that it had been owned by an Australian couple.

He got out of his car, wincing as his leg hurt, and tried to walk quickly to catch up with her. He knew where she was going. She always went to same place. It was a little café at the end of her lane. It was quite nondescript outside, and was never that busy either. Perhaps that's why she liked it. Maybe she did her deals here and that was why she'd bought the flat.

He'd popped into the café earlier in the week to check the joint out. He'd grabbed a sandwich and a bottle of water as he'd needed to take painkillers and they were so strong, he had to line his stomach first. He'd smelt the fragrant coffee, which made his body sigh with longing, but he'd already had one before work. He'd watched the owner for over an hour, without spotting anything out of the ordinary. It seemed to be a normal coffee shop. But he knew appearances could be deceptive – after all, Olivia looked nothing like a master criminal.

The café door gave a ding as he opened it and both Olivia and the man behind the bar looked up, then returned to their conversation. His heart was beating fast in his chest. He walked over to stand beside Olivia, pretending to peruse the coffee menu chalked onto a blackboard on the back wall. He was hoping to overhear what they were chatting about. The man stopped speaking, though, and turned to him with a smile, which was unfortunate. His two front teeth were missing. He would certainly stand out in a lineup. Gabe had wondered if Olivia would smell of cannabis or smoke, but the fragrance of coffee was so strong, all he could smell was a mixture of that and cake. His stomach rumbled and he realised that he forgotten to eat breakfast again.

He quickly ordered a muffin and a double shot of coffee and the man told him to go and sit where he liked and that he would bring the coffee to him. Damn. He'd wanted to stay at the counter, but he couldn't hang around like a gormless idiot.

He pulled out a chair near where Olivia was standing and tried not to stare at her backside. It was difficult, because it was pretty curvaceous. It made his mouth go dry and his hands start to sweat. He leaned in to try and hear what they were saying, but she started to jiggle about with the music that was playing softly in the background, and he was mesmerised. He'd seen her dance before on YouTube, but watching her gyrate a couple of feet in front of his face was enough to turn him insane. He looked around to see if the few other stragglers in the shop were watching her; they were. He gave them all evil looks and they turned away. He wanted to stand up behind her and cup her bottom in his hand, and whisper endearments in her ear, but she'd probably throw coffee in his face and stamp on his feet, or knee him in the balls.

He took a sip of coffee that had just been placed in front of him and almost choked. It was so strong. Spluttering, he felt firm hands on his back. Olivia was patting and rubbing him between the shoulder blades. She laughed as he turned to face her.

'That's Winston's coffee for you. I thought you were brave when you ordered a double shot. The coffee here is Winston's special brew. It's already twice as strong as normal. It's why I always have a latte. Then I start dancing to the music as I'm high as a kite,' she quipped and he almost spluttered again. 'Are you okay?'

He looked at her and she seemed to realise that she was still rubbing his back and sprang away. 'Sorry! I'm always forgetting personal boundaries. I rush to help people, whether they want my help or not.'

He held up his hands. 'It's ok. You probably just saved my life,' he joked. 'I think you should bring your coffee and sit with me, though… in case I keel over.' She opened her mouth to speak, probably about not talking to strange men, but he swiftly pulled out the chair next to him and she had little choice but to grab her drink and comply or appear rude.

Jackpot! He tried to curb his smug look in case he looked like a weirdo. He couldn't believe his luck. 'Thanks for the tip about the coffee,' he smiled as she brought hers over to his table. His eyes were sparkling with mischief and she grinned back. 'I could have done with it a few minutes earlier, though!'

He sniffed his drink and this time took a tentative sip, wincing again and reaching for the sugar. He sprinkled it in and swirled it around with the spoon he'd filched from the saucer of her latte. 'I never usually take sugar. Are you local?' He asked genially, his brain whizzing at a hundred miles an hour to find the best way to use this situation for his benefit.

Her eyes narrowed a fraction and they ran over him, as if analysing his words while she thought about what to say. That pause worried him a little. He sat up straighter and gave her a dazzling smile. She cocked her head to one side and took a sip of her coffee, her eyes never leaving his. He felt a drip of sweat slid down his back and he wriggled in his seat, his smile slipping slightly.

'I live not far from here,' she said after another taste of her coffee. 'How about you?'

'Just on the other side of town.'

'What brings you here today?'

This part Gabe had worked out. 'I've been visiting my nan,' he said. 'She lives in Hillview House, down the road. You probably won't know it, but it's not far from this coffee shop. I don't know how I missed this place before, but I guess I'm in a world of worry when I leave her. My feet walk me home on autopilot.'

Bingo! Her eyes lit up. 'I do know where it is. I visited it when I was looking for a home for my dad. They didn't cater for his specific needs, but I researched the place and it seemed really well run. Is your nan happy there?'

He smiled his first genuine smile of the day. Aside from possibly being a part of a criminal underworld, she had obviously cared about her dad. Perhaps that was how she paid for the swanky place her dad had stayed in? Gabe knew she'd sold the family home, but care homes like the specialist one her dad had stayed in cost thousands a week if you were paying privately, which she had. Perhaps that was why she'd started growing cannabis.

'Nan's happy enough. She's made friends she loves. She has round-the-clock care and I can stop worrying about broken bones. I know how much leg pain can hurt, from experience.' He lifted the cane by his side.

She smiled sympathetically. 'Is your leg hurt? Sorry, stupid question,' she slapped her forehead.

He laughed, showing his strong white teeth. 'It's ok. It's a rugby injury. The other guy came off worse.'

She grinned and seemed to be taking in his broad shoulders and muscly arms, which he couldn't help flexing for her benefit.

'Does this place ever get busy?' he looked around at the mostly empty tables.

'Only at the weekends. It's rammed with people then. The coffee is too strong for the mum crowd.' She gestured to the man behind the counter with his gangly frame and long hair. 'And Winston's wild look scares them off,' she whispered.

'Not you, though?'

Her eyes twinkled and he noticed green flecks in their depths. 'Not me. I don't judge people by the way they look. Winston is a complete darling. He opens up a night kitchen once a month for the homeless here. He's an angel.'

'You mentioned that your dad is in a home too? Is it nearby?'

Her eyes clouded over for a moment and she brushed the back of her hand across her nose and sniffed, making him instantly want to comfort her. He trod on his own toes to wake himself up from the trance she seemed to be putting him in. He smelt the air to see if she was wearing a perfume that was making his senses go wild. He wanted to scooch her onto his lap and nuzzle her neck to make her smile again.

'He passed away recently.' She spoke quietly and her head

dipped low, making her hair fall across her face on one side. It seemed the most natural thing in the world to reach out and brush her hair from her face. Then he covered her hand with his own on the table. She didn't push him away.

'I'm so sorry. I'd be devastated if anything happened to my nan. She raised me pretty much single-handedly.'

She raised watery eyes to his. 'Where were your parents?'

'Always working. They run successful businesses and I'm not sure having a child was part of their plan. How the hell it happened, when they organise every second of their lives, is beyond me. Luckily my nan stepped in and offered to help. I doubt I'd be here otherwise.'

She gasped at his honesty. He knew he'd got her attention and was working on her heartstrings.

'Are you an only child?' she asked.

'Yep. How about you?'

She hesitated for a moment, which made him frown and his senses go onto high alert. He made a mental note to do another background check. 'I am. I think I'd have liked a sibling at times like these, though.'

'Does your mum live nearby?' He already knew the answer to his question, but tried not to show it.

She sighed and slipped her hands from under his and placed them on her lap. His palm felt warm from her skin and he reached for his coffee and took a sip, almost choking again. She grinned, the tension ebbing away.

'She got ill and passed away when I was at primary school. My dad brought me up on his own.'

'That must have been tough.'

She had a faraway look for a moment, then drained her own frothy drink. 'Lots of single parents manage okay. My dad got Alzheimer's about ten years ago and that was the hardest part.'

'Hey, I'm sorry.' He genuinely was, this time. She smiled and his heartbeat ranked up a notch.

'It's not your fault. I blamed everyone for years, from the drugs he took for his back pain, to our family history, even his lifestyle choices. Turns out it was probably a mixture of factors. The drugs probably didn't play a part, but for a while I blamed everything.'

At the mention of the word 'drugs', his ears perked up. Perhaps she'd begun growing cannabis to help ease her dad's pain? 'Uh, sorry, I didn't ask your name?'

'It's Olivia. Yours?'

'Gabe.'

Her eyes crinkled up at the corner. 'That sound like an American cop.'

It was his turn to pause for a fraction of a second too long this time. *Shite.* Normally he knew better than to use his own name. But it was too late now. 'My dad's American, my mum's British. He won the toss about names. She wanted to call me Harold.'

'Thank goodness your dad won,' she joked. 'I used to have a pet fish called Harold and he was quite naughty. He used to play dead and almost gave me a heart attack a few times. Look I'd better go, I've got to get to work.'

He stood up as she did. 'What do you do for a living?' he asked with interest.

'I work with pens in a stationery cupboard,' she bantered, but he knew that it was actually true.

'Maybe I'll see you in here again sometime?' he called after her hopefully as she left.

'Maybe,' she said over her shoulder. She swished her dark hair out of her eyes and pulled the strap of her handbag further up her arm, her mind obviously already onto other things.

His ego took a battering. He might not be the most desirable man in the world, but he was used to female attention. He knew he looked good. Olivia hadn't batted her eyelashes at him, or laughed coquettishly like he was accustomed to. Finding women had never been hard, but for some reason his charm had failed him this time. He'd captured her interest by talking about care homes, but that had been part of his plan. The rest had been to woo her into getting to know him better and that had been an epic fail. He stared into his coffee cup, wondering what he'd done wrong, and noticed Winston looking at him knowingly. He came over, patted him on the back and put a fresh coffee in front of him without asking if that was what he wanted. Gabe smiled his thanks and shrugged. 'Do you know her well?'

Winston watched Olivia walk away through the window. 'Well enough,' was all he said before going back behind the counter and singing out of tune with the music on the radio. He served a man who had just walked in and asked for a Winston special, whatever that was.

Gabe sipped his coffee gingerly and felt it burn his lips. Winston laughed at something the man said and Gabe looked his way, but they were deep in conversation. Gabe grabbed some change out of his jeans pocket and paid up, thanking Winston and mentioning he would pop in again for more delicious coffee.

~

*W*inston watched Gabe leave out of corner of his eye. He made a mental note to tell Olivia that the man who had engaged her in conversation had been asking questions about her after she'd gone. You had to be careful these days and, after the few tricks Olivia had taught him and the women from the refuge, he knew they all had to stay vigilant about people who sought them out. They had to stick together. As the shelter was nearby, the coffee shop was a beacon for men to come in and ask about the women there. Winston would never betray them, or Olivia. He picked up the phone and dialed her number.

CHAPTER TWELVE

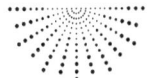

*O*livia had become a bit of an obsession for Gabe. If she was a criminal mastermind, then she hid it well. She hadn't been married or had lots of flashy boyfriends. She had dedicated her life to her father and giving him the best care possible. What he wanted to know was how the hell she had afforded it.

He rolled his shoulders and closed his eyes for a moment, trying to zone out the incessant hum of people talking into phones, or chatting to each other in the open-plan office. They did have panels at the back of their desks to give them privacy, but most people just leant on them as they walked past and stopped for a talk. He longed for his own office, but he'd been moved to this desk when he had messed up and got shot. It was his bosses' way of showing him exactly how important he was – not. So much for tea and sympathy.

He knew Olivia did work as a stationery supervisor, whatever the hell that entailed. Surely in a company the size of the one she currently worked for, people could walk over and pick up their own pens? He tried to imagine someone milling around his office with a clipboard to see if they needed any paper or pencils, but couldn't picture it. He guessed she must save the company money, though, or they wouldn't have employed her in the first place. You'd be pretty stupid to steal stationery from a police station, but it might happen elsewhere.

It looked like Olivia had worked for years, from the information he had on her so far. She had been her dad's main carer, until he'd had to move into the home. Gabe wanted Olivia's bank information, but he would have to explain why it was required and he didn't think a tipoff about some homegrown cannabis would be enough to swing it. He needed more than that.

Seeing an email ping into his inbox he clicked it, while wondering if Winston's extra strong coffee could have hallucinogenic effects. He couldn't stop picturing Olivia's breasts swinging the tassels around in her first viral video. It annoyed the hell out of him that millions of other people had seen it too. She seemed so modest in person, with her baggy T-shirts and nondescript jeans. She had a beautiful face and long sooty lashes framing inquisitive eyes, but her clothes screamed *don't look my way*. Maybe she didn't want to be noticed, unless she was on film? And her illegal activities would explain why she tried to blend in.

Scanning the email, he sat back suddenly and raked his fingers through his already mussed-up hair, trying to make sense of what he was reading. Taking his time to reread it again, he chewed his lip and started playing with a pen on his desk, before dropping it as if it was hot.

Why the hell was Olivia earning minimum wage, when she had the skills to net a fortune? He bet he knew what would be on her financials, when he finally thought of a pretext for getting them. In front of him was her employment history. She'd paid taxes in full and, until her dad had died, she'd been bringing in a fortune. From the digging he'd done, he could see that she'd grown up as an only child. Being isolated, it seemed she had turned computers for company and she was mostly self-taught. She had later taken lots of home-learning courses and was now a specialist in cybercrime. Would someone who helped people, like she seemed to, really commit a crime? Would she risk it all, growing cannabis in her own home? It just didn't make sense. Maybe she'd lost herself to grief after her dad passed away, and she'd fallen in with the wrong crowd. People often preyed on the vulnerable.

She'd run her own business from home and offered packages to big companies to protect themselves from hackers. He briefly thought of the person who was targeting and phishing people in the locality at the moment, but the idea drifted away, as it wasn't the right fit... for now. Unless that was how she'd paid for the big house she stayed at with the dogs. Had she been hurt by a man and this was payback?

Why work in a stationery cupboard, when you could probably run the company that you were working for? He rubbed his temples. This puzzle was starting to make his brain ache. The two pictures he had of Olivia just didn't add up.

CHAPTER THIRTEEN

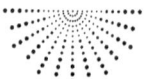

arius sucked the jam from his fingers and smiled at his mum. She grinned back and tucked a lock of her silvery blond hair behind her ear, the way she always did when she had something to say.

'You know I appreciate your help, don't you?' She sealed a few more jars from the latest batch of jam they had made and started sticking labels on them.

He knew what was coming. 'But?'

'But... you don't have to waste your time coming here making jam with me all the time.' She brushed her hand against his stubbly cheek and he leaned into it, almost sighing at the contact.

'I like helping you. Your jam ranges sell out every month and the money goes to the shelter.' Darius looked around at the industrial kitchen he had set up for his mum, in the women's shelter she ran. They worked side by side making jam in aid of homeless women, and it was a resounding success. Darius would happily have paid for the shelter to have all of the things it needed, but his mum still craved independence. He understood how much it meant for her to be the one providing for the amazing women that lived here.

'You should be out meeting girls and having fun, not counselling the broken women here and making them feel like you are the answer to all their prayers. They need to learn to protect themselves, Darius.' When he looked hurt, she wiped her hands on her apron before hugging him. 'They all adore you, but they're stronger than they realise. It's great that they now know there are amazing men like you out in the world – but they are all a little bit in love with your boyish good looks,' she nudged shoulders with him, or would have, if he hadn't been quite so tall. She ended up bumping arms instead. 'I want them to love themselves first.'

'I distract them?'

His mum laughed and reached up to stroke his face. 'With looks like yours, a woman would have to be dead not to fall in love.' She pulled his face towards hers and kissed his nose. Then she let him go and labelled the jar in front of her and handed it to him.

'Is this one for Libby?' he asked. He knew his friend hated people calling her by that name. For some reason, she thought 'Libby' sounded girly and weak. He thought it was a beautiful name – and he was the only one allowed to use it, now her dad had passed. He took the jam and put it in the grey rucksack next to him on the bench. He gave his mum a wry look and stuck out his tongue. 'She sends you her love.'

'I miss her.'

'She misses you too, but she doesn't really want to talk to anyone who reminds her of her dad at the moment.'

His mum's eyes filled with tears and she looked away. 'She talks to you.'

'That's different.'

'I know,' she sighed. 'Are you still hanging around together?'

'Not so much, recently. Everything reminds her of her dad. He used to be so proud of us, before his mind slipped away. Now she hates everything to do with work or play.'

'Give her time.'

'She's been doing dire jobs. She can't seem to stay away from tech firms, but she's doing work that she could do with her eyes closed.'

'Perhaps she doesn't want to think about anything for a while? She needs time to heal, Darius.'

'It's been months.'

'People grieve for a lifetime, son. Give it time.'

'How much time? I miss him too. He was a better dad to me than mine ever was.'

Seeing his mum flinch and turn her back suddenly made his heart ache. He had met Olivia at infant school when both were floundering. Libby's mum had just died, leaving her dad struggling to cope. Darius's mum had run away to the women's shelter, leaving him with a dad who drank and was hardly ever there. He knew how much his mum hated herself for leaving him there, but from visiting her at the shelter as an adult, he knew she'd had no choice. His dad would have killed them both if she had taken his son. He'd never laid a hand on Darius, and had tried to be a good dad for a short while after his mum left, but he'd slipped back to his usual ways.

His mum had begun to rebuild her strength at the women's shelter and, when she was well enough herself, she vowed she would return and reclaim her child. She had, eventually, but the years in between had been hard and he was almost grown.

Libby and her dad had become his family. They felt like outcasts together, from wearing clothes that were always too small to having jam sandwiches for dinner every day. Her dad hadn't been much of a cook. It was why Darius still sent

Olivia jars of jam… to remind her of their linked past and to show her he cared.

After a while, Darius's dad had begun to drink heavily again and Libby's dad had looked after them both. But he still had to work and that meant a lot of time alone. They'd discovered the Internet and gaming and had become enthralled. It was such an exciting time. They soon learned how to reach the world well beyond the walls of the house, and their families' means.

Libby hadn't liked the dark side of the web, but it drew Darius in. Not for the harm it could cause, but for the power he felt for the first time in his life. As they matured, Olivia used her skills to help businesses thrive. Darius had helped her originally too, but he wanted things brighter and faster than she did. She'd had amazing success for a while, but things had really slipped towards the end.

Darius had offered to pay her dad's medical fees – he could afford it. But Libby was so independent. She wanted to stand alone, while his only dream was to stand beside her. She just didn't, or wouldn't, see it. He'd make her understand, one day. She had no clue at the moment. He was watching, but was sick of her ignoring how serious he was about them as a potential couple. It was time for her to really stand alone if that's what she wanted, whatever the cost.

CHAPTER FOURTEEN

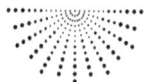

*O*livia rushed along the street and tried not to think of the broad shoulders and deep green eyes of the man she had met at the café. She'd agreed to meet Connie again, but had been strong enough to insist they met halfway this time. Olivia got there early and ordered two frothy coffees and a round of toast and jam. She thought fleetingly of Darius and the jam he sent every month. He said it was from his mum, but she knew he'd helped set up the business. It was a really successful cottage industry and it kept the shelter afloat. Olivia was proud of the way he supported his mum, even though he'd been left at the mercy of his dad. She loved Joan, but she wasn't sure she'd be as forgiving as Darius was. Olivia was the one who had held his hand when he cried for hours after his dad gave him yet another whack around the head. She was the one who persuaded him to go with her to the doctor when the ringing in his ears hadn't stopped for days.

Olivia wasn't sure she would have been so gracious, but then the only memory she really had of her mum came from her dad. She knew how much Darius loved his mum, but

Joan had the shelter. To Olivia, she still seemed to be putting others before her only son. Olivia was his stability and the only person he trusted completely.

Any other girl would die to have a gorgeous, tall, dark-haired, thoughtful, adorable man like Darius love her, but Olivia could never quite give him what he needed. She did love him. He was the most important man her life now, but they saw the world in different ways. He was a crusader. She saw herself as more of an invisible woman.

Looking up, she noticed Connie opening the door and peering around, searching for her. Olivia watched the other patrons of the café with interest. A few customers flicked a glance Connie's way, but it seemed that being over forty made most women invisible. People thought you had passed your prime, so failed to notice you half of the time. Olivia's younger years had been spent caring for her dad or working to pay fees for his care, so now, finally, this was her chance to live her life for herself, instead of for someone else. The problem was that she felt she had no real purpose without her dad. She felt his loss to her core. Even though he'd lived somewhere else for years, not only physically, but in his mind, she had always hung on to glimpses of the man he used to be.

Connie spotted her and waved before heading her way. She was wearing smart trousers and a blouse in a soft taupe colour. Olivia would have loved to have seen her in something bright and snazzy but Connie's view on snazzy was probably a bit different to Olivia's. The thought made Olivia snicker and she covered it up with a sip of her coffee, greeting Connie with a coffee moustache again.

Connie bent down to kiss her on both cheeks, apologising for being late, and giving Olivia time to brush the foam away. 'Thank you for meeting me again.' She sounded breathless, as if she'd just run all the way there, but Olivia had a sneaky suspicion that she just been driven by a chauffeur. Olivia had seen a big black car that was a bit posh for this area pull up outside.

'It's ok,' said Olivia, biting off a corner of her now-cold toast, but enjoying it anyway.

'What did you find out?' Connie asked.

Nice to see you too. Olivia realised she must have rolled her eyes, since Connie's cheeks flushed.

'Sorry! I should have waited at least a minute before I asked that,' she said ruefully.

Olivia relaxed and smiled. Maybe the whole 'we hate Greg gang' idea wasn't the best. 'It's okay. How are you?'

'I've been better. Every time Greg speaks to me I want to scream at him and smack him in the face, but he's so irritatingly reasonable about everything. He's being nice to me again and wants to make love all of the time.' She pulled a grossed-out face. Olivia made a face too, but quickly hid it behind her coffee cup before her new friend saw. He was still Connie's husband, even if he was a sex-mad gigolo who was after his wife's money. It felt nice that another woman was turning to Olivia for advice. She'd never really had that before. She hadn't had time for a girlfriend. People never seemed to understand why she stayed in all the time, and didn't go out meeting men and clubbing. That scene wasn't for her.

'He's been buying me gifts and flowers and wants us to plan an exotic holiday. Perhaps we were wrong about Jen?' Connie continued.

'Um... we might be.' Olivia remembered walking in on Greg and Jen the other day, after she had obviously just given him something to smile about. She could tell from the way he'd turned away quickly and straightened his clothes, while Jen couldn't hide the smug grin on her face. Olivia had backed out rapidly. She couldn't say she'd seen anything specifically – but she knew. 'Have you changed your mind about looking?'

'I think so,' so sighed Connie. 'Maybe I overreacted? I was a little bit hormonal and possibly made you think something that just wasn't there. I'm not usually the jealous type, but after that second bottle of wine at the Christmas party, I went a bit psycho. Greg's always saying I imagine things. I think I'll back off for a while.'

Olivia felt her stomach drop and rubbed her hand over it, which just made it hurt more. She personally thought that Greg was a thoughtless dumbass, but she wasn't married to him. It wasn't her problem. She grieved the loss of her first proper girly friendship in years. Connie would have no use for her now.

'One good thing has come out of all this stress, though,' said Connie, her eyes twinkling. Olivia's shoulders slumped as she crunched her toast, dropping crumbs everywhere. Connie swiped them away and continued, grinning and nudging her arm. 'I met you! I'm so bored with my family dictating who they think I should hang out with. You're much more fun. I feel empowered when I'm around you. I hope you feel the same?'

Olivia's eyebrows shot up. She almost choked on her last bite of bread, while a glow of warmth filled her belly. This beautiful, vivacious, if rather misguided, woman wanted to be her friend.

'I know you might think I'm a bit flaky,' Connie went on. 'But Greg said Jen is an octopus. He's had a word with her and threatened to move her to another department if she bothers him again.'

'Well…' said Olivia slowly, her brain going into overdrive at how to handle this turn of events. How could she tell a woman who was so obviously in love that she thought her choice of life partner was a scumbag, without destroying her? This was uncharted territory for Olivia. Her gut instinct was to tell Connie to kick him in the balls and throw him out. 'If you are absolutely sure that's what you want and you think everything is good with you and Greg, then I support you, of course. I know how much you love him, from the way you talk about him.'

Connie chewed on her lip. 'Is it too much?'

'Not at all.' Olivia admired Connie's perfectly painted soft pink nails and vowed to get a manicure. She just had to save up first. 'It's great that you adore the person you're married to.' Even if it is Gobshite Greg, she fumed silently. She'd stopped calling him Gorgeous Greg as soon she'd found out he was married. It hadn't seemed appropriate any more. Especially now that she was best friends with his wife.

Connie drank her coffee and grinned. 'Are you busy?'

Olivia looked at her phone and wished she had a full diary to check. She had sorted out her pens for the day and even entertained the dogs.

'Um… not really.'

Connie squealed and clapped her hands. 'Let's have a girly day out. We could get a manicure,' she said, tutting at the tiniest imperfection on her nails. Her face lit up. 'We could even get our hair done?'

'Uh,' Olivia glanced down at her own chewed nails. 'I can't remember the last time I got my nails done. It could be fun…' For the first time in ages, something unfurled in Olivia's chest. She'd been walking through fog for months, but suddenly it was clearing.

She wished she had a proper job again, with a good wage. Every penny she'd ever earned had gone on private health-care for her dad, but once he'd passed away, she couldn't see the point of working so hard. Now, she realised she could have used some of that money to start living again for herself. She squeezed her eyes shut and refused to let the tears flow. Her dad would be horrified to see the mess she was now. He'd bought her up to be an independent woman who could look after herself.

She thought of the minimum wage she earned at the stationery cupboard, together with the amount she got for her few hours a week with the dogs, and totted up some numbers in head. She bet Connie didn't frequent places that slapped on a coat of fluorescent varnish for a fiver, but she reckoned she could actually afford a file and polish, even if she wasn't making the kind of salary she'd been used to before. Apart from a couple of coffees at Winston's café, she hadn't spent much of her meagre wages. 'That sounds great. I'd love to.'

Connie's eyes lit up and she slurped the dregs of her coffee, ignoring the cold toast. Olivia was tempted to grab it to eat on the way but, after one longing glance, she left it on the plate.

$\approx$

*F*our hours later the women emerged from Connie's favourite salon in Chelsea, primped, polished, plucked – and, in Olivia's case, broke. It was as if had she slaved away for two months and then thrown the money into a fire, Olivia thought. Her mane of thick, dark, shoulder-length hair had been trimmed. It wasn't much different – unlike where the stinging from her private area was making her walk like a cowboy. She had been mortified when Connie said they were also booked in for a wax, as it had been like a forest down there. Not any more! Now it was a swollen and sore desert. Ouch!

While she was being groomed she'd had time to think about her financial situation. She couldn't believe she had just spent hundreds of pounds to leave her hair looking almost the same as before, and as for the soreness down there... She glanced at her crotch. Was this what girlfriends always did? Perhaps she'd had the right idea, staying away from all this. She thought of her only other friend, Darius, and the way his hand slipped proprietorially from her back to her waist, and then she shook her head to clear the picture.

'Hi!' Connie touched her arm, making her jump. Her silky mid-tone blonde hair had been highlighted and cut and looked divine. Her make-up had been skillfully applied, her nails were glossy pink and perfect, whereas Olivia's were the colour of mud. The shade she'd chosen had appeared beige in the varnish bottle, but dried a sludgy tone. Just her luck!

'How did your waxing go?' Olivia whispered, leaning towards Connie, and wincing in pain. Connie laughed, eyes twinkling. 'Oh no, I didn't get that done. I just get a top-up every month, but I heard Jane saying they went the whole hog with you, you brave girl. Did it hurt?'

Olivia blushed at the thought that they had all been talking about her private parts, but she gritted her teeth and smiled manically. 'Not at all! I just haven't been for ages, what with my dad dying recently.'

Connie blanched and leaned on the salon wall for support. 'I didn't know your dad had died. I'm so sorry.'

Olivia's eyes narrowed, but she saw that Connie was genuinely upset.

'I'd be devastated if anything happened to my father,' Connie continued, tears forming in the corners of her eyes. She grabbed Olivia's hand and squeezed it in sympathy.

Olivia's bones suddenly felt heavy. 'He was unwell for a long time. He had Alzheimer's and drifted further away from me every year.'

Connie pulled her into a hug, almost knocking Olivia off

her feet. It felt good to be held by someone who didn't want to jump her bones.

'Let's go and order a lovely lunch and you can tell me all about it,' Connie said.

Olivia had always wondered what it would be like to tell someone other than Darius about her life, but now she had the opportunity, she felt reticent. Could she trust her new friend Connie with the real her, or would it shock and scare her? Deciding to give friendship a try, Olivia let Connie lead the way and gingerly pulled her jeans from her groin, wincing again and slowly following her up the road.

CHAPTER FIFTEEN

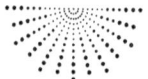

*G*abe hadn't had much time recently to look into the cannabis growing tipoff. He had received loads of complaints from people who'd had their bank accounts hacked and had been learning more about how the mystery hacker preyed on men who had mistreated women. Most of the men wouldn't come forward officially, as it might point the finger at their own misdemeanours.

He was now less inclined to believe it was a criminal group, and thought it might be a lone wolf. The profiling seemed really personal. The men were humiliated at having fallen for a scam, even though it was so well thought out that Gabe reckoned most people would fail to ascertain that they were being conned until it was too late. He guessed that was the whole point. The Damsel hacker didn't pick his targets indiscriminately. These people were targeted. The scams were getting so realistic that it was difficult to seperate the real banking documents from the fraudulent ones.

He hated listening to some of the targets, or victims as he should call them, drivel on about losing money, when he'd already had complaints filed against them at some point in the past. It was hard to be sympathetic when they had hurt other people. Bloody hypocrites. He was even feeling empathy for the Damsel hacker, after he'd had to sit with two pompous men moaning on about how something had to be done.

The hacker had a trick of siphoning off the bank accounts of men who posted photos of their exes online. The money was taken in tiny amounts at first to see if it triggered a response, then more went after a period of time. Sometimes vast sums were taken. The targets were usually rich and quite often had a history of violent abuse against women. Occasionally, the hacker seemed quite mischievous, trying to get the men into trouble. Things might be ordered on their accounts. One guy had received a delivery of ten horses to his flat in Mayfair. It caused mayhem and the press had become involved. But when Gabe did some digging, though it was hard to prove the connection, each and every target had a female victim in their past somewhere. Gabe was sure it was one person behind the whole operation. A group of professional criminals wouldn't bother messing around, they would make their message clear from the start.

Staring into his coffee at Winston's café, he realised he had almost become accustomed to the bitter taste. He looked up as he heard the café door open, and then held his breath as Olivia walked in. She was wearing a new top that molded her breasts and scooped low across her chest. It was a deep inky blue and matched her fitted jeans. It looked like she had been shopping and, although the tones were muted, they made her figure sing. He watched her hips sashay to the counter and saw Winston's eyes light up at the sight of her.

Her shoulders were a little straighter than the last time and he wondered if she was coming to terms with the loss of her dad. Everything he had dug up about her screamed loner. She had dedicated herself to her father, to the detriment of her own life. It seemed that the only significant person in her life was the boy she had grown up with. He hung around a lot, although he hadn't been seen at the big house to date. He was at the flat often, though. Gabe had tried to find out more about him, but his dealings seemed to be legitimate. He ran a property portfolio, amongst other things, and did very well judging by the fast, flashy car he drove and the cut of his clothes. Gabe hadn't been able to get much further. He was one good looking dude, though, and Gabe supposed that they might be together, from the amount of time he spent at the flat. Gabe's own house was actually only a fifteen minute walk from the coffee shop. Olivia's flat was in plain sight in the street opposite, so he'd become a regular and usually sat by the window, watching the road.

In the end, he'd had to decide that the person who had tipped him off about drugs had been delusional, and he'd shelved that report. He hadn't seen any hint of drugs going in or out of the big house and he'd staked it out at various times of the day and night. For some reason, he still found himself coming to the coffee shop to check on Olivia. It was on the way to visit his nan. He knew first-hand how having an elderly relative you adored going into home could make you feel both relieved and guilty at the same time. He felt emotionally connected to Olivia, even though they had only met once.

His leg was healing well, but he'd taken to bringing his cane into the coffee shop in the hope she recognised him. He was getting desperate and was even contemplating tripping her up and making her fall into his arms, when he decided to try something more direct. 'Olivia,' he called out.

She looked up in a daze and then frowned when he held up his stick. 'Oh hi. Sorry. I was in a world of my own. Gabe, isn't it?' She had remembered his name! He'd only asked hers as she'd left last time.

'That's right.'

'What brings you here again?'

'I was working nearby, but the job fell through, so I came to sample the amazing coffee,' he joked. Olivia grinned and walked over to peer into his coffee cup to see if he was actually drinking the bitter liquid. 'It's an acquired taste, but I like it.'

'Tough guy,' she joked, a touch of admiration in her voice.

'Join me?'

She looked around to see if he was talking to someone else. Then she shrugged and signalled to Winston to bring over her a frothy coffee with extra milk and a piece of squidgy coffee and walnut cake. She pulled out a chair and sank into it gratefully as Winston placed her drink and a delicious-looking slab of cake in front of her. With a wink, he put down two spoons.

Olivia flushed and pushed the plate into the middle of the table between them, breaking off a morsel of cake and tipping it into a mouth, closing her eyes in bliss and sighing. Gabe felt his abs tightening and his mouth go dry. What was it about this woman?

'I didn't expect to see you in here again after the face you pulled, last time you sampled the coffee,' she joked. 'Try it with a mouthful of cake.' He did, and his eyes bugged out at the sugary bliss. The coffee almost made him feel like he was on a high. She giggled and her eyes sparkled with mischief.

'What the hell is in this stuff?' Once he had swallowed it he smiled. 'I knew there had a to be a secret as to why you came here and drank the coffee.'

She paused for a fraction of a second then giggled again, swiping some cake right off his spoon. 'I didn't know you well enough to tell you before. Winston's baking is sublime. It makes up for his coffee. It's why this place is rammed at weekends. His coffee and cake together are out of this world but he likes the place to be quiet on the weekdays. It means the women from the shelter around the corner are more likely to pop in. They can be a bit nervous, understandably.'

He enjoyed seeing the warmth in her eyes. 'You mentioned the woman's refuge last time. Do you have friends there?'

'They're all my friends. My best friend's mum runs it. I help out when I can. I haven't been there for quite a while, though.' She pushed a piece of cake around the plate. 'Not since my dad died.'

'I'm sorry for your loss,' he reached across and took her hand and she didn't pull away. 'I'm sure they understand.'

'I'm not convinced they do. My friend keeps hassling me to go back there, but I can just about deal with my own problems and haven't got the emotional energy I need to be able to help them.' He gave her hand squeeze and reached for his coffee. He grimaced and rapidly stuffed a spoonful of cake in too. She smiled sadly and followed suit.

'Perhaps they would like to be able to return the favour and help you?'

She frowned, as if this hadn't occurred to her. 'How's the cake?' she asked, changing the subject. He noticed that her nails had been freshly painted, but wasn't sure about the brown colour. He had only ever seen her wear pale colours or white. The underwear he'd seen on the dog video was a deep pink, but she usually covered her curves with plain white T-shirts. Perhaps today was the start of a new her.

She saw him notice her nails and fanned her fingers on the table. 'My new best friend persuaded me that I needed a fresh look and some sizzling new varnish.'

'New best friend? I need one of those. My friends keep making fun of my walking stick.'

She giggled and gave him a sympathetic smile. 'She says I've been neglecting myself since Dad died. She's actually my boss's wife.' When he raised his eyebrows at this, she seemed pleased. 'I thought the same as you. Why would the boss's wife run around with someone who works in a stationery cupboard?' she paused for a second and tilted her head to look at him. There was mischief in her eyes. 'For some reason she does. I think she's lonely, as her husband's a moron.'

Gabe spluttered on his coffee and she put a hand over her mouth to control her giggles. 'Sorry, I'm always doing that, speaking before I realise what I'm saying.'

'Don't apologise. I wasn't thinking that at all. Why wouldn't she want a friend like you?' Gabe wondered if this boss's wife had been on the list of connections he had been asked to look into at work, but didn't think so. Then he remembered the case of the cannabis in the big house had been closed anyway, and signed off as a hoax. A woman like Olivia could own more than one property if she wanted to. She could even ignore her great palace of a house and sleep in a tiny flat if she chose. She was grieving. Who was he to tell her where to sleep or what to buy? Although he did wonder where she'd got the money for the house from. That wasn't in the financials he'd finally been given, but the house was definitely hers. His interest was piqued once again, but he tried to let it go.

'Connie – my friend – invited me for a whole spa day, but I've never been to one before. When I came out, I was almost bald!'

Gabe looked at her glossy hair in confusion and she burst out laughing, not explaining what she meant. He liked the sound of her laughter.

'Sorry. Private joke.' Gabe frowned again and then pictured where else she might be bald and... bingo! She chuckled into her coffee.

He tried to smother a laugh. 'A spa day sounds posh.' She

sighed deeply for a moment and the fabric across her chest pulled even tighter. He really tried not to stare.

'It does, doesn't it? The problem is that Connie is a bit posher than me. I'm not grand at all. In fact, I was so nervous I rambled on to the hairdresser the whole time and probably made her ears bleed, when I was supposed to be relaxing.'

He laughed and she smiled. 'Perhaps you need some practice at putting yourself first for once?' She sighed again and ate some cake, making him wish there was more to share to keep her there longer. Where was Winston and fresh cake when he needed him? His coffee was cold now which made it even more bitter. He heard Winston whistling from the kitchen and winced, trying to block out how off-key it was.

Olivia grinned. 'I'm not really a relaxed sort of person.'

'Me neither. Maybe we should learn?'

Olivia's big brown eyes twinkled at the suggestion and she ran her hand through her hair, making it swish around her face.

'What are you doing tomorrow?' he asked her.

'Nothing. I should be cleaning my flat as it's the weekend, but it can wait. Why?'

'Let's see if we can find the most chilled thing to do on a weekend. What is the first thing comes to mind when I say the word relaxing?'

Olivia chewed the side of her lip and concentrated by squinting her eyes and shredding a napkin in front of her on the table. 'Lying on a Lilo on the beach?'

He pictured the local beach and its freezing water. They'd been having gale force winds on the coast and he pictured them both stranded on rocks somewhere, shivering, teeth chattering. 'Hmm, that might be bit cold. How about the local swimming pool?'

She looked horrified. 'Last time I went there I was five.'

'They have an adults-only evening. We can sit in the

Jacuzzi.' When she was about to object, he reached for her hand. 'It will help my injury no end.'

'I thought you just said it was improving?'

'The Jacuzzi will be good practice for that spa day.' He didn't mention that he was actually already picturing her in a bikini. She bit her lip again and looked at the pile of shredded tissue, then her eyes creased at the sides and she grinned.

'Why not? As long as you let me buy you a drink afterwards to ease your poor eyes after the shock of seeing me in a swimming costume.'

'That's the bit I can't wait for,' he said cheekily, and she blushed. He went and grabbed another napkin, filching a pen from Winston and writing his phone number down on it for her. 'It's a date.'

'A date?' she squawked, brushing hair from her eyes and pulling her jeans up at the waist, which made her breasts wobble interestingly.

'A date,' he said firmly, walking over to kiss her on the cheek. Then he exited the coffee shop before he embarrassed both of them by kissing her soft pouty lips, the way he'd wanted to for the last half an hour.

He felt alive for the first time in ages. Whoever had called into the police station about the big 'hot' house had done him a massive favour. Both he and Olivia were single, and both lonely by the sound of it. Perhaps they could help each other lift the gloom they had been in for far too long. Plus, she was as sexy as hell. He'd never seen a woman as unaware of herself as Olivia. He couldn't wait to get to know her better.

He would have to decide whether to come clean about his job or not, but there was still an outside chance that she *was* doing something dodgy. If that was the case, she would run once she knew what he did for a living. He didn't want that. He felt alive for the first time in a long while. It wasn't just about sex, although before meeting her he had suspected that his libido had gone to sleep with his leg. He was pretty sure women didn't want a useless man who limped and couldn't keep up, so he'd stayed away from them all and got angrier and angrier with himself for not healing faster. With Olivia, he wanted to bite her skin and nibble his way down her body. His lap was already uncomfortable and he moved his trousers to accommodate the growing bulge, a big smile on his face. He was glad his car was near or he might scare someone. He put his hands in his trouser pockets, whistling as he walked, forgetting about his cane. He should be working, but instead he was racking his brain for an intimate little bar he could take his date to, after their swim.

CHAPTER SIXTEEN

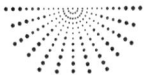

*O*livia walked away from the coffee shop feeling a bit weird. It seemed she had a date with a seriously hot man and she couldn't quite understand how it had happened. He wasn't new to the area, as he'd said his nan was in the home nearby, but she'd never come across him before. She would have remembered if she had. But perhaps she had been walking around in a fog since her dad died and not noticing anyone, while thinking no one noticed her. She was such an idiot.

Speaking to Gabe had brought butterflies to her stomach… and swimming? What the hell was all that about? Perhaps she should put him off. Then she remembered his leg and wondered if he needed someone to go with him, to help motivate him to relax more. He had called it a date and been adamant about it, though.

The problem was that her hair would probably go frizzy in the water and she'd end up looking like a scarecrow. She wondered if there were swimwear sites for curvy girls so she wouldn't feel too out of place. She wished she hadn't eaten a whole box of crunchy nutty cornflakes for dinner the night before, washed down with a mini bottle of Prosecco. She didn't usually worry about her soft curves, she loved them, but Gabe was seriously sexy! Man, he had muscles. The dimples in his cheeks when he smiled made her head feel funny and her insides fizz, even before she'd touched any wine.

She rushed through her front door and mentally tallied her bank account. Connie's excursion to the salon had almost cleaned her out, but at least her lady garden was tidy for swimming. She hoped that it didn't start to grow back too quickly and start looking like a spiky forest. She couldn't recall if they had set a date, but then a message pinged. It was a text from Gabe. They'd exchanged numbers earlier, even though she'd got a disapproving stare from Winston. Winston was wary of new people, as sometimes men came looking for the women at the shelter. She'd given him some tips on how to spot people from out of the area. It was a bit similar to poker. People always had some sort of tell. But Olivia had sat and had a coffee with Gabe, so Winston should know he wasn't a threat.

It was a good job that Darius hadn't been around or he'd have gone mad. He was always banging on about security and safety. She knew she hadn't been on the ball lately, but she could tell if a man was genuinely interested in her – and Gabe was. She was pretty sure Gabe could pick any girl he wanted, but for some reason he was fascinated by her. He stared into her eyes as if she was the only woman on Earth and made her heart tremble. She sent up a silent thanks to her dad. She and Gabe had a common interest. Perhaps other women didn't understand the obligation and love he felt for his nan. In the past, friends hadn't understood why she didn't leave her dad to rot in the care home. That was why she now had so few. She hadn't needed anyone, except for her dad and Darius, until now. Connie had opened her eyes to having a proper girlfriend, and Gabe was a delicious distraction.

She picked up her phone to call Connie and got an excited squeal when she told her about the gorgeous man she'd just met. Darius would just have growled at her and told her he was after one thing, but Darius hated anyone she got close to. She thought about it for a moment and wondered if that was another reason why she didn't have friends. She frowned and parked that thought for later, as Connie was nattering on about coming to the flat and bringing some costumes over for Olivia to try. She had a pool in front of her summer house at home, so she owned lots of swimsuits. Olivia tried to protest, but she was broke and about the same size as Connie, so why not? Connie insisted on coming straight over, which made Olivia slam down the phone in despair. Her flat was a disaster zone!

She wondered if she could pretend the big house with the dogs was hers, as the home owners were never there. But knowing her luck, they would be home for once and she'd get sacked. Again. Then she remembered having told Connie her real address when they were at the hair salon. Her neighbours would have a heart attack, seeing Olivia having an actual visitor other than Darius. She hoped they were home to witness her glory.

She checked that she had snacks and wine, as Connie seemed like a girl after her own heart where food was concerned. She felt like she had pressed a button and gone into superspeed, shaking out the bedspread and throwing a blanket across the end to make it look a bit posher. She picked up a handful of work clothes and shoved them to the back of the wardrobe. Whizzing into the little lounge and kitchen, she washed down all the surfaces and threw a couple of scatter cushions back onto her couch. She usually sat on them on the floor, to paint her toenails. Looking around her clean flat, she realised how tiny the space was. In pride of place was a photo of her, her dad and Darius, taken when they were camping by the sea one year. Darius's own father had left him home alone while he catted about with his latest girlfriend, so Olivia's dad had called him and left an angry message, and then scooped the kids up for a week in a camp-site beside a pretty beach. It had been magical. They had eaten hotdogs on the warm sand, and stayed up late gazing at the stars. It had cemented their bond as a family.

Darius had been as devastated by her dad's illness and death as she had. He was the only person who almost always understood her. He didn't condemn what she did and she didn't tell him off too often either. She wished he earned a living some other way, but who was she to judge? He was a result of his circumstances. She blamed his dad for the way he was now, although there had to be a point when he stepped up as an adult and took responsibility for his own choices. She understood what he did and why, but he was clever enough to make money another way. He just chose not to, and that was where she found it hard for them not to fall out.

Hearing the flat door buzzer, she pressed the intercom to let her guest into the building, not bothering to check who it was and trying not to run to the door in glee. She was supposed to be a cool sophisticated lady, not a desperate freak. She pulled her door open and was shocked to see Darius standing there.

'Darius! What are you doing here?'

He grinned wolfishly and pulled her into his arms, looking into her eyes. She couldn't help but grin back, before he planted a smacker on her lips.

'Uh… Olivia?' came a tentative question from behind his wide shoulders. They turned in unison, but Darius kept hold of her. Olivia cringed inside. Connie would think she was a complete strumpet. She'd only told her she'd just met a new man about twenty minutes ago. She pulled out of Darius's embrace and shoved him into the flat.

'Hi Connie!' she said brightly, as if snogging a gorgeous man on her doorstep hadn't just happened.

'Is that Gabe?' hissed Connie, a bit too loudly, her eyes running over Darius's backside, as he walked into the kitchen and started making coffee as if he owned the place.

Olivia laughed over-gaily. 'No, that's Darius.'

Connie's eyes were out on stalks. 'Darius? I thought you said the smokin' hot guy was called Gabe?'

'Gabe? *Who* is Gabe?' Darius asked, turning round, eyes piercing into Olivia's like lasers. It was at times like this she wished her flat was bigger. Olivia glared at his possessive tone and ignored him.

'Come in, Connie.' She stepped back to invite her friend in. She was glad that Darius was there to distract Connie from the tiny size of the flat. 'This is my best friend, Darius.' He rolled his shoulders and looked at Olivia for a moment, before running his eyes over Connie and making her blush. He seemed satisfied, gave her a wink, and went back to making coffee.

'Oh, wow!' Connie hissed. 'That man is gorgeous! And I just saw him kiss you. Why the hell do you want a Gabe when you have a Darius?'

Olivia sighed. 'It's complicated.'

'I wish my life had complications like that,' said Connie, pointing a perfectly manicured nail at Darius's pert backside, clad in designer jeans. Olivia slumped into her seat.

Even she didn't really know why she couldn't take Darius seriously. He dated lots of women, but she knew it was only because she pushed him away. She didn't know what he saw in her, but she just didn't love him the same way. She adored him, but sex with him could destroy everything. If it didn't work out, she would lose the only person in the world she cared about. She couldn't risk that. She needed him. She wished she loved him the way he loved her, but he was a bit obsessive about her and that confused any feelings she could have let grow.

Olivia smiled at the way Connie's eyes followed Darius as he placed the mugs of steaming coffee on the little glass table by the deep blue couch. He kissed Connie's hand, making her mock swoon. She ran her eyes all over his tall frame, inquisitive eyes, and his beautifully cut, thick black hair. 'Nice to meet you,' she said, still gawping. Darius grinned. He was used to having that effect on women. He especially liked to preen in front of Olivia in hope of making her jealous, but she just rolled her eyes.

He sat next to Olivia on the couch, so close that she was practically sitting on his lap. The couch was small and in the end she moved to sit at his feet, where he immediately started massaging her shoulders, which was so amazing that she was loath to tell him to stop.

'So who is Gabe?' he asked again, a slight edge to his voice. Connie giggled like a schoolgirl, then said, 'he's the guy Olivia met in a coffee shop down the road. He's asked her on a swimming date.'

Darius's hands paused, then started to rub Olivia's shoulders a bit harder. She flinched, before he realised what he was doing and stopped.

'You're going on a swim date? Since when? You hate swimming.'

'I'd go on a swim date if a gorgeous man asked me to,' said Connie and she winked at Darius. His lips set in a thin line.

'It's a shame that you're married, then,' said Olivia, and then regretted it as Connie's skin flushed a deep shade of pink. Connie paused for a moment but recovered quickly. Olivia could have kicked herself for behaving like a jealous freak. Now she knew how Darius felt when she met anyone, and resolved to be kinder to him.

'My husband runs the firm Olivia works for,' said Connie. 'We met at the works party and became good friends.'

'Connie has kindly offered to let me borrow some swimming costumes,' Olivia said, smiling at the woman to soften her previous remark. 'The last time we went swimming we were probably about six, Darius.' She nudged his knee affectionately, but he didn't smile.

'I'd have taken you swimming if you'd wanted to go,' he said petulantly.

She hugged his leg. 'I know,' she said soothingly. 'But Gabe has an injury and he needs to heal, so he asked me to join him.'

'Is it a date?'

'Um…'

'Of course it's a date,' said Connie happily. 'He sounds divine. What did you say he did again? How did he hurt his leg?'

'Um…'

'You didn't find out?' Darius's eyes narrowed and she felt pinned to the floor. Her face went bright red.

'I don't need a full background check on everyone I date, Darius,' she said feebly. She looked at Connie, who was still staring at Darius. 'He thinks that since my dad died, it's his responsibility to take care of me. I'm a grown woman. I can take care of myself.'

'I know you're a grown woman.' He gave her a heated glance, his eyes running over her body, until she got up to go and find some wine.

'Let me take you both to dinner,' he said from the other room. 'Invite your husband if you like,' he said Connie.

'He's out of town on business,' she said slowly, and Olivia wasn't sure if either of them believed this. She had heard that

Jen had two days off work and she wanted to kick Greg firmly in the nether regions for the way he treated Connie. Olivia knew Darius wanted to show off but perhaps Connie needed some fun, especially while Greg was off doing goodness-knew-what.

Connie looked unsure, as if the thought of going out without her husband had never crossed her mind before. 'It could be fun, but where would we go?'

'Darius can get us in almost anywhere. Where would you like to go?' Olivia could almost see Connie's brain picturing seedy nightclubs and crappy burger joints. She felt a little affronted that Connie would assume that of her and her friend – but then Connie hadn't seen him anywhere but this flat. Darius's penthouse apartment was probably bigger than Connie's house, but she could find that out in her own time. For now it might be fun to let her squirm a little.

Olivia didn't go out with Darius much, as he always insisted on paying. Every penny she earned had previously gone towards her father's care. Now her wages were ridiculously small. She didn't have the energy to make money the way she had before. She had wanted a job that she could almost do without having to function fully. Now, though, she was just beginning to think that maybe there was a world of options out there for her. She knew she could earn the big money that she had before, but she could also change direction with the new plan she'd had. It was just a seedling of an idea at the moment, but if she nurtured it, it could grow into something amazing. She just needed to keep Darius's nose out of it, and beautiful Connie seemed like the perfect distraction. They both deserved a bit of fun.

Connie still might not want to believe that her husband was a liar, but she could enjoy the attention of an Adonis like Darius for an evening. Darius had a way of making women feel like they were the only person in the world. Connie could do with a bit of mindless flirting to build her confidence. Then perhaps she would see that there were other men out there that were way better than serial cheater Greg.

'I promise to take you both somewhere nice,' said Darius, not wasting an opportunity to drag Olivia out of the flat. 'It's my treat.'

'I couldn't do that!' said Connie, looking around the small flat in panic.

Olivia laughed. Darius had more money than Connie could ever dream of, even though she was loaded herself. He'd have paid for Olivia's dad to live in a palace if she'd let him, but she had been determined to look after her dad on her own, the way he'd looked after her all those years when she'd been growing up. It was her responsibility. He'd been a wonderful father. She squeezed her eyes shut for a second and then felt Darius's arms slip around her. She sank into him gratefully as he kissed the top of her head. He always seemed to sense when she was thinking of her dad. Then he reached across the couch and kissed Connie on the lips, making her mouth hang open, as he got up to leave. As he sauntered off, he called out that he'd send a car for them both in a few hours. Olivia walked over and gently lifted Connie's chin to close her mouth.

'He's a lot to take in, isn't he?'

'He's sending a car?'

Olivia nodded and grinned. 'He has a business twice the size of yours,' she said gently.

Connie's mouth dropped open again. 'Why the hell haven't you dragged him to the altar, when he's so obviously besotted with you?' she asked, almost angrily.

Olivia had asked herself the same question a million times. She still didn't have an answer. She'd loved him with nothing, and even with money, he was still the same person inside. She wished again that she could love him the way that he loved her. Perhaps a date with a good-looking man like Gabe would awaken her lady parts and make her begin to appreciate all Darius did for her and all he offered. But Darius wanted to be her whole life, and she wanted freedom. She'd been ruled by circumstances beyond her control for so long that she was fighting back. Her new life would be on her own terms.

The thought of Gabe made her skin grow warm and start to tingle, so to distract herself, she opened up her computer to show Connie where Darius would probably take them. She enjoyed the look of surprise and delight on her friend's face, as Connie picked up her handbag, left the swimming costumes in a pile on the couch, and rushed off to go and primp and pamper herself for her joint date with a very hot man.

Olivia's one long black stretchy dress would have to do for this occasion. She hadn't let Darius coax her out for a long time and she knew how much he loved her in that dress. He'd bought it for her, after all. He hated her usual T-shirt and jeans combo, bemoaning the fact that she wouldn't let him take her shopping or order online on his account. Perhaps she should have let her principles slide occasionally. She knew he wanted to take care of her, but it was about time she started to care for herself.

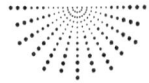

*G*abe was working. He hated going to places like this. He was still on the trail of the hacker, who had recently drained the bank account of a well-known businessman who frequented this club. After speaking to the business owner, Gabe had decided he was a pompous idiot, but those being targeted still had a right to assistance. Each case was highly sensitive; the press getting word of anything could cause major embarrassment. He was pretty sure the hacker counted on that. No one was prepared to risk exposure and the amounts didn't make a dent in their fortunes in the grand scale of things. The Damsel hacker wasn't greedy enough to wipe the targets out completely. He was just teaching them a lesson they wouldn't forget.

Gabe decided to visit a few places this latest victim was a patron of, to try and work out some sort of pattern. Perhaps he'd been set up by a member of staff somewhere, or a customer. It could even be someone in their business network who was linked to local information technology firms holding their financial data. Gabe's colleagues were tucking into free beers and getting totalled, but he wanted to keep a clear head. He smiled as his friends commented on a group of stunning women who had just sidled up to the backlit bar and propped their backsides on the silver stools in front of it, long legs and high heels dangling enticingly. His eyes slid sideways as a woman with jaw-dropping curves walked through the door in a sculpted cream dress. She fitted right in with her blonde hair, expensive clothes and the bling dripping from her neck and wrists. The man with her was tall and good-looking. They were a handsome couple, but the man was facing slightly away from him. As the man moved to the bar, the woman sitting next to Gabe stopped talking and gazed at the male newcomer, suddenly sipping her drink seductively and playing with her hair. Lucky bastard. Gabe remembered the days when women looked at him that way, but since the accident he knew he scowled and frightened them away.

He vowed to try and be a nicer person. A picture of Olivia came into his mind. He blinked as he realised she was actually right in front of him – she was a vision in a fitted black dress that scooped low across her shoulders and gave a glimpse of her breasts. Her dark hair was pinned to one side with a sparkly adornment. His heart almost felt like it had stopped in his chest.

He blinked and open his eyes, watching her lean in and laugh at something her companion said. She was with the glamorous couple and he now couldn't tell which woman was with the man. Gabe felt his blood start to boil, even though he had no claim on her whatsoever. Why had he assumed she had no life, when she had that huge house? He had no idea, but the woman he had conversed with just a couple of times seemed a world apart from the one in front of him now. That woman had dressed to blend in, not to stand out like the woman here. Her dress clung to her curves and Gabe couldn't take his eyes off her.

She looked up and their eyes met, Olivia's going wide in shock and Gabe's showing a glint of fire. She dropped her hand from the other man's back and just stared at Gabe, whilst her female companion noticed and followed her gaze across the room.

Connie giggled and touched Darius's arm. 'There was me thinking that Olivia might be a bit lonely, when I first met her. How wrong can you be? That man looks like he literally wants to eat you alive, Olivia.'

Darius had been giving their order at the bar but he immediately stopped and his head whipped round. Olivia flushed and appeared like she wanted to run and hide, but Gabe had already told his friends he was going to chat to someone. He got a friendly joshing for finally talking to a woman, as his colleagues grinned in Olivia and Connie's direction.

Gabe knew from her file that Olivia wasn't married, but he'd hoped she was single when she'd agreed to their date. He wasn't about to play second fiddle to anyone. He crossed the bar towards her, not giving her any time to make up excuses or escape.

'That's Gabe,' said Olivia almost breathlessly. Connie gasped and clapped her hands, whilst Olivia looked like a rabbit caught in headlights. The man next to Olivia didn't look too happy either, so Gabe guessed he wasn't with the blonde woman, then felt a punch of recognition as he realised it was her friend, Darius.

As he approached, Olivia smiled, but it didn't hold the warmth of the woman he'd met earlier and his stomach started to hurt. He held out his hand to Darius. 'Hi, I'm Gabe. Hi, Olivia.'

Darius had no choice but to shake his hand. 'Darius,' he replied, sliding his arm around Olivia's waist. She moved to introduce Connie, which put some distance between them, giving Darius no choice but to drop his hold.

'I didn't expect to bump into you again so soon,' Olivia then said, looking nervously at Darius.

Gabe leant in and kissed Connie's cheek, making her giggle. Olivia took a sip from the champagne-filled glass that had appeared on the bar.

'Connie is my boss's wife and Darius is my best friend,' Olivia explained, but at Connie's sudden pout, she corrected herself. 'Sorry, Connie. I'm not used to having girlfriends. Meet my friends Connie and Darius.'

Gabe's mood lifted considerably and he wondered why Darius was scowling now, if they were just friends. He quickly understood it was because friendship wasn't Darius's choice. Gabe's mood became even better. He motioned to his colleagues across the bar. 'Would you like to join us all for a drink?'

Olivia glanced across at his friends, who were watching them with interest, but shook her head with what seemed like genuine regret. 'Darius and I are treating Connie to a big night out and we're just starting with one drink here. Thank you for the offer, though.'

Darius gave Gabe a victorious stare and he shrugged his shoulders, locking eyes with Olivia. 'Ok. I'm looking forward to our date in a couple of days, so I guess I'll have to wait for that.' She gave him a sweet smile and this time her eyes twinkled, making him draw in a deep breath. The notes of her floral perfume tortured his senses when she leaned towards him and gave him a kiss goodbye.

His friends gave him a roasting about chatting up a woman who was already with a better-looking guy, but for once Gabe couldn't wipe the smile from his face. Olivia was looking forward to their date! He also pointed out that the women they had just bought drinks for were all staring at Darius too. They scowled good-naturedly and joked about upping their game.

CHAPTER EIGHTEEN

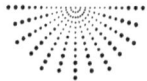

*O*livia strolled about in a bit of daze. She filled up pen pots and was ignored by her colleagues as usual, but she really didn't care anymore. A few weeks ago, this mindless job had seemed important. Even helping Connie in her ridiculous plot to get revenge on Greg had appeared realistic, but now she could see Connie felt confused.

Outside work, Greg was playing a blinder, and he was doing the same at work too. Now he knew Olivia was on to him, he was far more circumspect with Jen. The way the girl moped around with a face as long as the Eiffel tower, Olivia guessed that Greg might have even dumped her. Perhaps he already had his sights set on another poor sucker. He had a short attention span, it seemed. Meanwhile Connie was full of energy and had discovered that she could have a good time without Greg, thanks to Olivia and Darius. It looked as though Greg had suddenly realised his wife might now enjoy life on her own terms, and he had panicked.

Connie was her friend, but she could be a bit cloying, Olivia had discovered. Plus she was a grown woman. She could sort her own life out. If she wanted to turn a blind eye to her husband's cheating, it was up to her. Everyone's relationship was different and who was she to say what would, or wouldn't, work out. Olivia thought about the screwed-up notes Jen had written him, which Olivia had retrieved from the bin by Greg's desk, but decided to leave well enough alone. If Connie was happy, so was she.

She thought back to her date with Gabe the night before. It had been a bit awkward when they'd both stood there in their swimming costumes. She'd ended up embarrassing them both even more, by walking up to him and bending down to touch the wound on his leg before she had even said hello! The scar was healing, but it looked worse than a mild rugby injury.

He'd grabbed her hand to cover his discomfort and led her to the Jacuzzi. Another couple was just leaving and they exchanged smiles as they settled into the bubbles. The Jacuzzi was half screened by tall leafy plants and she was thankful they hid her shyness at wearing such a low cut and embellished swimming costume. It was beautifully designed and made her feel sexy, but was a bit glitzy for her taste. It was better than many of the others Connie had left with her, though. Some were almost indecent.

Gabe had asked her about her day, and her jobs. He'd frowned when she related some funny stories about dog sitting and described the house, though. Perhaps he thought it sounded crass. She didn't know what had come over her next, but he'd put his hand on her knee while he was talking, so she leaned closer to hear what he was saying. Before she knew it, they were kissing and barely coming up for air.

If she'd thought it would be weird kissing someone she hardly knew when they were both wet and half-naked, she was so wrong. He ended up pulling her into his arms and she didn't hold back or care who could see them. His lips had been tempting and delicious and her hands had run along his back and met firm muscle. It had been a long time since she'd felt this wanted by a man. She'd given herself up to it. He'd groaned and had to put some distance between them, as he was breathing hard.

They'd looked into each other's eyes and then burst out laughing – they were behaving like horny teenagers. He stood up after a while and joked that she'd taken his leg ache away. He leaned on her as they went to get changed and then pushed her into one of the changing cubicles and shut the door behind them. He pressed her up against the door with his slick body and kissed her again until she was panting his name.

She was distraught when he pulled away again, his eyes glazed. He reluctantly said they should stop before they got arrested. She giggled and came down from the sexual haze that always enveloped her when he was close by. She reluctantly slid her hands out of the back of his swimming trunks and let him go, so that he could go to the next cubicle and get changed. She closed the door behind him and breath wooshed out of her.

She'd thought it would be awkward after that, but he had been waiting outside for her. She had quickly washed and blown her hair dry and tried to cover her sweaty face with make-up, but he stood there looking hot in jeans and a white shirt molded to his chest, which made her want to weep tears of happiness at the sight of him looking so damn sexy.

He'd held out his hand to her and they had walked up the hill into town in dreamy silence. She hardly ever went into the centre of town, it wasn't much fun on your own, though she knew it could be bustling and welcoming when you had company.

Gabe led her to a little bistro and bar where they'd fed each other delicious spaghetti in tomato sauce, washed down with a rich bottle of red wine. When it was time to go home, he'd walked her back to her flat and kissed her outside until her lips were plump and rosy. He hadn't asked to come in and she hadn't invited him, but he mentioned he'd like to see her again. She said truthfully that she was looking forward to it.

Darius had kissed her a few times when they'd been out drinking, but it had never felt like this. It had been years ago, but she felt that he was building up to something lately and it probably involved her. Darius was so sure that he knew what was right for her. But kissing Gabe had opened up a whole new world of possibilities that she hadn't known existed. She'd enjoyed sex before, but never felt lightning from her fingers to her toes like she did when Gabe touched her. His body called to hers like a drug.

She wanted to phone Darius and tell him she'd actually felt something for the first time in years, as he was her best friend. He told her about the incredible women he met and casually dated, but somehow she knew he wouldn't feel happy for her, the way she did for him. Connie was the first woman for years who'd made her feel a twinge of jealousy around Darius.

Now she looked around the office, straightened her shoulders, and grinned gormlessly at her colleagues, who gave her strange looks as they walked past even faster than usual. A new woman had started working on a desk near the stationery cupboard, and everyone avoided her too. Olivia wandered over and said hello. The woman almost jumped out of her skin, before offering her a shy smile. She looked to be in her late thirties or early forties, with a mop of long red hair that seemed like she'd run her hands through it a thousand times. Olivia's own hair was surprisingly much easier to manage after the extortionate trim Connie had persuaded her to have. It hadn't felt like they had done anything at all, but the treatment they'd slathered on – and almost got in her eyes – still made her hair fall like a glossy waterfall round her face.

The stylist had thrown the half-used tub of cream in the bin by her feet after her treatment, and she'd shoved it in her bag before she turned round. Olivia had been using it sparingly and the results were amazing. She felt like she could be a walking hair commercial. Shame about the rest of her, but she was working on that too. She was thinking more about her appearance and how she had shrunk away from people for so long, avoiding eye contact wherever possible. Suddenly she wanted to be bathed in light and to enter the real world again. She yearned for people to notice her.

Olivia would have invited the new girl to lunch, as she knew what a minefield the work café was, but she only worked a few hours a day. Her fingers felt like they had come alive again and she was itching to get back to her one true love, the keyboard.

Even though the computer in the stationery cupboard was a relic, it still functioned perfectly. The powers that be had given high tech machines to most of the staff, but hers had minimal data on it and was just for tallying stock levels. She'd downloaded a free programme and tightened up all the stock inventory, which had already saved the company thousands. In a company this size, the issue had been overlooked, a mistake in itself. The company accounts were updated regularly, but the stock total wasn't investigated. They'd soon start realising how much stock everyone took home for personal use – particularly stationery – once she added her programme to the main system.

She could have flagged it up, but why bother? Olivia quite liked knowing something they didn't. She knew she shouldn't play with the computer that sat on the little wooden desk against one wall of her walk-in cupboard, but who made people work in an environment like this? They could easily have made a space for her in the main office. Instead she was closeted with walls of pens and paper for company, in a tiny 'office' without windows. Greg had recently offered her an alternative, but only because she was now his wife's friend. She sat at her desk and her hands felt like they had come home as soon as they rested on the keyboard.

She tapped away happily, occasionally glancing over her shoulder towards the door, but no-one really knew she was in there. She plugged her tiny hard-drive into the side of the computer and logged easily into the company mainframe. Within minutes, she had a wealth of information at her fingertips. Seeing her mobile phone flash a message from Gabe, asking if she was free that evening, she calculated how much time she was required to spend with the dogs, did a mental checklist of everything else she needed to take care of now that she was back in the land of the living, then sent a response to Gabe saying she'd love to.

She pictured her sad-looking wardrobe and decided that she'd had enough of being skint. Although she'd managed to save a tiny amount, the visit to the salon with Connie had wiped that out. If they were going to stay friends, then they'd have to tone down their social calendar a bit. She thought of the extra money that she'd saved the company in expenses and how that figure would look in her own bank, but that wasn't her style. She wasn't that desperate… yet.

She decided that she needed to stand up for herself more. Connie was wonderful and popped round every few days, but hadn't yet invited Olivia to her own pad. Maybe she thought Olivia would knock things over or make the place look messy. Olivia imagined it must be like a palace.

She shut her work computer down and sent some emails on her phone. As expected, she started receiving replies almost instantly. Instead of the pressure she'd felt before, adrenaline was buzzing around her veins and the excitement at getting back to her own career was growing.

She had tried working for someone else for minimum pay so she didn't have to think, but she knew her dad wouldn't want that for her long term. He'd been proud of everything she'd achieved. He would have been furious at how much money she'd spent on him over the years if he'd realised, but she'd never said a thing. His comfort had been her priority. Now he was gone, perhaps she could carve out some of that for herself?

She grinned when she thought of what Greg and her colleagues would think if they found out what she actually did for a living. Perhaps they would raise a smile her way or invite her for a coffee? Then she wondered if she actually wanted them as friends in her real life. Probably not. They would bore her to tears within minutes.

CHAPTER NINETEEN

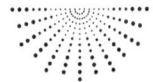

*D*arius watched the figures in his bank account grow. He was an astute businessman and could often forecast trends. He read voraciously and made sure he hung around in all the right places, keeping his ear to the ground. He sighed and rolled his neck, to ease the tension in his back. It had been building for weeks now. Only Olivia knew the real him, not the one he presented to the world. He didn't ever show that person to anyone, especially his mum. He was getting tired of trying to be the perfect son to Joan, though. After all, she had left him at the mercy of a drunk. Then he chastised himself. She'd done what she had to, to survive.

Olivia was one of the only people who'd kept him going during that time. The crush he'd had on her since school had blossomed into love as they'd grown. He knew he should back off and give her space, but he couldn't. She infuriated him. He'd assumed that, when her dad died, she would turn to him, but she'd withdrawn from him completely. She was just out of his reach.

She'd met Connie and seemed happier, but now Gabe was

sniffing around. That was Darius's fault, too. He'd been angry and wanted Olivia to ditch her crappy jobs, so he'd done something stupid, which he now regretted. He knew exactly who Gabe was – a policeman – and why he was on the prowl. Olivia was at the heart of it because of him. Darius had thought he could jump in and save her, or persuade her to work with him again, but it had backfired and now Gabe was in both of their lives.

He thought of the new woman who had just arrived at the shelter his mum ran. She'd been emotionally and physically battered by her boyfriend and was shaking when his mum had introduced them. Now her eyes lit up when she saw him and she'd gradually trusted him with her story.

Darius looked at the screen in front of him and saw pictures of her and her boyfriend on holiday. He'd accessed her boyfriend's private files directly from his computer and spent a few hours finding out everything about him. Darius looked at the man's browser history and found out where he worked and the places he frequented. Darius grabbed screen-shots of a few documents and photos. He had enough money to last a lifetime but, now Gabe was on the scene, he needed to be extra careful. He had lots of stocks and shares that were carefully invested to make sure both he and Olivia were always comfortable, whether she protested or not. She didn't have her dad around to take care of her, and that was his job now. He hated her working in that pen cupboard, but she was stubborn. He'd waited long enough and he was blowed if he'd let someone like Gabe stroll in and hit on her. Darius would get to her and tell her who Gabe really was first.

Darius wanted to make Olivia understand what he did for other women, so she wouldn't be so hard on him. He knew she let him live his own life, but she didn't like the way he did things. She thought she knew better, and that she could help people without humiliating those who had hurt them. He disagreed. It was time these people paid for the way they treated women like his mum. Olivia was usually careful about who she worked for, but she'd let things slide since her dad died. Darius had missed his chance to tell her who Gabe was, though. He'd just have to keep trying to persuade her to find a new job, or to go back to her old one.

He winced and downed his coffee, which was watery and a bit cold. The bone china cup one of his staff had presented it in almost broke, as he slapped it down on the desk in his secret office. This part of his huge penthouse apartment, on the top of one of the city's best-known buildings, was well away from prying eyes. Most elite places had safe rooms these days. This one housed his computers and work stations. It was concealed behind a wall in his bedroom and fitted his needs perfectly. He mostly worked on his laptop while sitting on his bed, as it afforded views across the sea, just outside the town. His work was solitary, which was why he liked staff in his flat, and enjoyed checking in with the almost-real world with Olivia. It had been so much more fun when they'd started this idea together. Then she'd backed out and gone all serious and law abiding on him. He'd shown her how they could make serious money from the people they were targeting, but she'd gone solo and made vast sums on her own.

It was as annoying as hell. He didn't have the patience to shoulder her workload. But he made far more in a shorter time. Who was the smart one now?

CHAPTER TWENTY

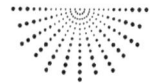

*T*he dogs jumped up and were so pleased to see Olivia that she was actually finding it harder and harder to leave them behind each time she visited. She knew she'd have to quit this job soon, as her old one was all-consuming. Perhaps she should find time for a proper home and dogs. The house owners still kept this place like a furnace, but the stupid games and costumes for the dogs had stopped. Perhaps it had been some sort of test to see if she would actually do as they said, and now they'd got bored.

She eyed the small camera in the corner that was still flashing its tiny red light. She stuck her tongue out at it, but hid her movement at the last minute. Maybe the owners were perverts? She'd noticed the camera soon after she'd first arrived here, but assumed it was a good way to keep an eye on the dogs. She'd never seen the camera move and had guessed it was a static one which pointed to where the dogs slept. There weren't any cameras in the rest of the house, so that must be why it was installed. She sat on the couch and let the dogs jump all over her before they calmed down. They gazed adoringly at her. She loved them now. It would be heartbreaking to give them up. She made another quick decision about her future, hugged the dogs to her, then got up to walk outside and make a call to a local dog shelter.

When she got home, to her annoyance Darius was there, and so was Connie. Darius had let himself in. Then Connie had arrived. She could never be cross with them for long, so she flopped down next to them both on her couch, with her head on Connie's shoulder and her legs across Darius's lap. It was funny how comfortable they had all become with each other in such a short space of time. She thought Connie had a crush on Darius, but he seemed to be enjoying it, so who was she to complain?

'Where have you been?'

'At work. Make yourself at home, why don't you?'

Connie giggled and Darius held up a wineglass for her. She took it and slurped a big mouthful. 'Why are you both here… in my flat, instead of your own homes?'

She saw a flicker of hurt flash in Darius's eyes before he masked it. 'We thought we'd take you to dinner as a surprise. You've been working hard lately.'

Olivia tried to be angry at him but it was impossible. She was glad to see them both. Today had been difficult. She was finding it harder and harder to leave the dogs, as they cried when she left now. At her other job, Greg had started to pay her more attention, which was disturbing and exhausting. He was starting to make her feel uneasy around Connie, through no fault of her own. She did love the idea of a night out with her two best friends, though.

'How was work today?' asked Connie, her head slumped back on the couch, before she pulled herself up and almost spilt her wine. 'Are you coming to dinner with us?'

'It was fine. Gabe sent me a text earlier today to ask me out,' she said apologetically. Connie cheered and clapped her hands, seemingly genuinely happy for her. Darius glared at her and sipped his drink, eyeing her over the rim of his glass. She could literally see the cogs of his brain whirring sometimes.

'How much do you actually know about Gabe?' he asked.

'She knows enough to have snogged the face off him,' snorted Connie, sending red wine flying in every direction from her nose. Olivia frowned and wondered how many glasses of wine Connie had already had. She used to have the odd bottle of wine in her kitchen, now it looked more like an off-licence, as Connie brought bags of it with her every time she visited, which was often.

'How long have you two been here?'

'Long enough to drink a bottle of your cheap plonk,' giggled Connie, forgetting that the wine was from her own house and sloshing the dregs from her glass onto Olivia's couch.

At first Olivia winced, then she quickly realised that she really didn't care that much about her bland couch, and shrugged instead, ignoring the growing stain. She scowled at Darius. 'Are you trying to get her drunk?' she accused him. Darius held up his hands in surrender as Connie tried to nibble his ear across Olivia's chest. Olivia noted that he only half-heartedly pushed her away.

'She arrived here drunk. I sent you about five texts.'

Olivia pictured her phone in her bag, and cursed that she been so eager to get home and pamper herself a bit before her big date. She hadn't bothered to check her messages. She'd been sent so many emails now she'd told people she was back at work, that she had slid the button to silent earlier on. The constant ding of notifications had got a bit much. She had forgotten how in demand she had been before she'd decided to change jobs and dropped off the edge of the planet. She knew enough about tech to be able to stonewall them all, and that's what she'd done. Only Darius knew where she was now. She'd have to make some fast decisions about who to work for first, now that she was back in the land of the living.

She leaned across Darius, smelling his familiar aftershave, one that she'd bought him, and heaved Connie up into a sitting position again. 'What happened?'

When Connie just swigged the last of her drink and laughed, Darius rolled his eyes. 'She thinks that her husband is cheating on her again.'

There wasn't really censure in his voice, just exasperation. Olivia knew he quite liked Connie, but this really wasn't his problem and she wasn't one of his shelter women. She might be upset, but she wasn't destitute or homeless. Olivia saw Connie blanch as she pushed herself up to go and find more wine in the little kitchen. Her usually immaculate hair was all mussed up and out of place, and it looked like she'd done her make-up in a hurry, forgetting to blend half of it in.

Olivia followed her into the kitchen. Connie was opening and shutting cupboards and tutting in disgust when she only found odd food items and no more wine. Olivia opened a low cupboard behind the door and pulled out a bottle. Taking Connie's hand she let them both back to the couch, where Connie fell onto Darius's lap. He lifted her off and placed her next to him. The three of them sat knee to knee, bottoms squished into one small couch, facing the flatscreen TV. It was the one item she'd brought from her old house.

Olivia slid down onto the floor and turned to face Connie. She was now drinking directly from the wine bottle and Darius gently took it from her. Olivia's stomach cramped. He had that look about him that he had when he decided to 'help' a damsel in distress. She could just picture him envisioning ways to make Greg pay for embarrassing his friend with his wayward loins. That wouldn't help Connie at all, as Greg was the director of her father's company. It would embarrass their whole family and possibly destroy the careful marketing around the company that Connie part-owned. Plus if he lost money, so would Connie. They probably had a joint account. Darius really needed to think this knight-in-shining-armour thing through.

'What makes you think he's cheating, Connie?' she asked gently. Olivia might be fresh to being a girl's best friend, but was going to try her hardest to help Connie in any way she could, even though she only had exactly one hour to shower, wash her hair, paint her nails and get dressed up for her very hot date. She pictured the pretty top she had bought on her way home from work after a detour into town. She wished she'd thought to buy some new shoes, instead of the plain black boots she always wore at this time of year. Mentally chastising herself for not concentrating, she tried to listen to Connie's drunken ramblings and held her hand. Olivia really hated Greg right now. Her beautiful friend deserved way better.

'He's been ignoring me again. He went away for a weekend and was lying about the hotel. He said he was staying there on his own,' she reached for the wine and Darius gave in and let her have the bottle before she suffocated him with her chest. 'When I called them, they said he was there, but was at dinner with a colleague.'

'Maybe it was a client?' Olivia reasoned.

'But he's started getting his back waxed, and I saw a receipt for a manicure and pedicure! I bought him a cute little kit and he always used that before. He's never been for a manicure in his life. I rang the salon to ask if he'd left his wallet there, and they said they'd check in the massage rooms. Massage rooms? It sounds like a sex shop!'

'Connie,' soothed Olivia. 'Lots of men like Greg want to keep looking good with therapeutic massages and facials nowadays. It's a posh hotel by the sounds of it.' She noticed

Darius's hand on Connie's leg and tried to ignore it. He stuck his tongue out at her. 'It won't be a sex shop. He probably wants to look his best for you. You look younger than him,' she said truthfully.

'He's just had his hair dyed, but I liked the distinguished look,' said Connie, her voice raising an octave. Olivia frowned and Darius chewed on his lip.

'Look, you need to find out more about all this,' he said.

'No, Darius,' said Olivia firmly.

He rolled his eyes heavenward. 'I was going to say, before I was rudely interrupted, didn't you ask Libby to keep an eye on him before? I'm sure she would be happy to do that again.'

Connie's eyes lit up but Olivia held up her hands. 'No. I'm not cut out to be a spy.' She gave Darius an evil look. 'Plus, I think you need to confront him yourself, if you think he's doing it again, which I'm sure he's not.'

'Let's take Connie out to dinner and we can all talk about it,' said Darius.

Olivia's eyes narrowed. Was he trying to scupper her date with Gabe? Darius pulled a face to protest his innocence, inclining his head towards Connie who was waving her wine glass in the air and mumbling how confusing it was that Greg wanted somebody else, as she was a goddess. Darius laughed and took the wine away again.

Olivia remembered reading somewhere about 'girl code,' and knew she should definitely put her new drunk friend before her own love life – but the memory of Gabe's hands on her waist and his lips on hers made her push herself up off of the couch. She needed to get ready, but still she hesitated.

'Gabe can come with us,' Connie spluttered, trying to hoist herself up but only succeeding in falling on top of Darius, which he seemed to be enjoying. Olivia reached out and pulled her up.

'I don't think so.'

'Great idea!' said Darius, swiping her phone before she could stop him and sending a message to Gabe.

'How do you know my new password?'

He smirked and ignored her at first, but she stared him down. 'You're becoming complacent, plus I always know the password to your phone. It's the only place I can get in. You hide everything else from me.' He was sounding as whiny as Connie.

'I need some privacy from you! You promised you'd stopped interfering.'

'I have…'

She didn't believe him, but let it go for now. Her phone pinged with a response and she made a grab for it, but Darius held it up high and then read the answer. 'It says, where should we meet?'

Olivia looked at Connie, who was standing on wobbly legs and pulling up her designer jeans so that they went too far up her crotch. Olivia cringed and gave in. 'We need to sober her up. Let's go to Winston's theme night. He's decided to try to get more custom by opening at night and this evening he's serving chilli and rice.'

'Have you ever tasted Winston's chilli and rice?' asked Darius, hiding a smile. 'It's like his coffee – enough to take the roof of your mouth off.'

'That's why we should go. I'm taking a couple of jars of marmalade your mum made. Apparently if you add something sugary into hot chilli, it cools it down.'

'You love Mum's marmalade!'

'I know. The sacrifices I'm willing to make to help Winston's café succeed,' she said through gritted teeth. She wanted to kick him. 'Come on. You wanted to interfere with my date, now you have. You'll also have to distract Winston and Connie while I sneak into the café kitchen and tackle the chilli. Gabe can help me.'

Darius gave her an evil look but she ignored him and went to find Connie's shoes, quickly slap some make-up on herself and swap her top. She'd gone from looking forward to a night out, to dreading it in the space of an hour, and it was all Darius's fault. She was sure he could have looked after Connie on his own for a while.

CHAPTER TWENTY-ONE

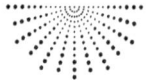

*G*abe didn't really know what to think when he got the text from Olivia. It had been brusque and short and mentioned a change of plans. He was usually a sociable guy, but lately he'd become a bit grumpy and his previous date with Olivia had made him crave more. She'd left him dazed and panting. He hoped they could find time for more of those exciting kisses, and this time she might even invite him in for coffee.

He was curious about so much. He wanted to see more of her, but he also needed to get a look inside her flat. He'd forgotten to tell one of his colleagues that he'd shelved the cannabis enquiry. She had finally handed him a set of financials on Olivia that morning. It appeared that she had been paid huge sums of money in the past as a consultant by lots of prestigious firms, including some banks.

The hairs on the back of his neck had stood up and he'd gone to stare out of one of the windows at work, watching people scurrying about on the streets below. Usually the view soothed him, but today he was too busy connecting the dots. A woman who worked from home for some of their country's biggest institutions… someone who could access bank accounts. The fact that she paid cash for that huge house that she didn't even live in. And some of the high profile targets of the Damsel hacker had accounts at firms she dealt with. Could she be the thief? He recalled that she'd also lied to him and said she just worked at the house with the dogs. Was that because she didn't want him to turn up there?

He was so distracted that he stubbed his toe as he walked past a colleague's desk. She laughed, telling him he probably got shot because he wasn't looking where he was going. He bit back a retort, hoping that his sore toe and damaged leg would carry him to his computer without him having to use his cane in front of her.

Why was Olivia working for the minimum wage at an IT company? Why had she been sacked from her last two posts? He pictured the way her eyes dilated when he kissed her and recalled the small noise she made in the back of her throat after he slid his hands from her waist to her backside. He threw an old coffee cup from his desk into the bin. There had to be an answer. Even if it meant he had to hang around with two of her friends, then perhaps it was worth it. He'd know more by the end of the night.

He walked up towards Winston's café and was pleased to see it was buzzing with people. Customers were fanning their mouths and laughing. He squinted through the glass. It looked like Olivia was waiting tables. He opened the door and walked over as fast as his leg would let him. When he kissed her cheek, her skin flushed a fetching shade of pink. He offered to take a couple of plates for her and was glad he'd left his cane in his car, however much he had to grit his teeth as he walked.

'Sorry about this,' she gasped. 'But it's much busier than Winston anticipated. He thought he might get a couple of locals, but the women from the shelter have turned up in force and so have a whole busload of pensioners, whose transport broke down half an hour ago. I got a frantic phone call from Winston and we all rushed down here.'

He looked at her top, now liberally splotched with chilli, and grinned. 'Don't worry. I'll help you. Tell me what you need me to do.'

'Marmalade!'

'Marmalade?'

'Yes. I brought a few jars with me. I knew Winston's chilli would make grown men cry. Look at that guy over there,' she tilted her head at a tableful of excitable men and women. One man literally had pouring sweat from his bald head. Everyone was taking it in turns to dab his forehead with napkins, which he seemed to be enjoying.

'Shove a jar of marmalade in the chilli in the kitchen.'

'A whole jar?'

'Yes. He's made mountains of the stuff and it will cool it down.'

'Will Winston mind?'

'I'll get Darius to distract him.'

'Where is Darius?' He looked around busy café and wondered how the hell they would cope with this full house. He paused for a moment. This wasn't his problem – but it could be fun.

'He's in the kitchen, trying to stop Connie from drinking a whole bottle of Scotch.'

'What? Oh hell, don't worry. I'll go and find the marmalade.' She was already getting on with serving, but he dropped a swift kiss on her plump lips while he had the chance. She focused on him for a second and smiled.

'Thanks.' It was the sweetest smile. He headed towards the kitchen and found Darius wrestling a bottle of whisky from Connie. They both froze when they saw him.

Gabe didn't really know what to say. 'Are you okay? Olivia asked me to put marmalade in the chilli as everyone's sweating.' They giggled and Gabe shook his head, but started smiling too. 'She said you need to distract Winston, Darius.'

'Ok,' said Darius. Connie was wiping her hand across her eyes and had sat down by the oven. On the shiny glass hob was a big pot of bubbling chilli. It smelt amazing but all of the spices in the air made Gabe's eyes water. 'The jars are just over there,' said Darius. 'Keep an eye on Connie.'

'But...' Gabe didn't know Connie well enough and, once her drunken giggles had died down, she seemed visibly upset about something. Perhaps Darius had broken her heart? Then he remembered Olivia saying that she was her boss's wife.

Darius patted him on the back as he left the room. Gabe looked cautiously at Connie. She was sitting dangerously close to the bubbling pot. She gave him a watery smile and put out an arm for him to lift her up. She wasn't the lightest of women and he staggered slightly. She wasn't helping him at all. She was half-lying on his shoulder and half-sniffing his aftershave and mumbling that he reminded her of her husband, before she started to sob and slip onto the floor. Olivia chose that moment to come into kitchen and she took in the situation immediately. She grabbed Connie around the waist and was soon making soothing noises. She manoeuvred her back onto the chair, which she nudged further away from the oven with her foot. Then she grabbed the jar of marmalade from the side and upturned the whole lot into the big pot, stirring it quickly, never taking her eyes off her friend.

She glanced at Gabe for a moment. 'I'm so sorry about this. Connie's had a family crisis and we couldn't let her be on her own. Her husband is out for the night and she decided to enjoy a few drinks with friends. I think she'd already had a bottle of wine before she even got to mine.'

'I'm sorry to hear she's upset. Is there anything I can do to help?'

Olivia shook her head. Gabe watched her stir the chilli and then they all jumped as Winston and Darius came into the kitchen. 'What are you doing in here?' asked Winston, his eyes darting between them and then resting on Connie, who was quietly singing now. Olivia and Gabe looked at each other guiltily.

'Sorry, Winston,' said Olivia, moving to take Gabe's hand. 'We'll clear out of your way and I'll help you serve up.' He peered into his chilli suspiciously as they backed out of the room, grabbing Connie and half-carrying her between them, trying not to snigger.

Gabe was enjoying himself. He liked the way Olivia looked after her friends, and tried to ignore the way Darius touched her as he passed in the doorway. They handed Connie over to a table of women from the shelter, who immediately found her a bowl of chilli. They listened carefully as she told them her woes. For the next two hours Olivia, Gabe and Darius were rushed off their feet serving customers.

As the last customer left, they sighed and kicked off their shoes. They waved goodbye to Darius's mum, who had agreed to take Connie home to the shelter with her for the night. Before that, Connie had hugged everybody and kept slurring that she was going to shed her old feeble persona. After talking to so many of the women and hearing their stories about fighting to live a normal life, she'd offered the shelter a donation of thousands of pounds. In the end, she had passed out in the corner and spent the last hour snoring loudly. Joan and a few of the women had had to practically carry her out, after refusing assistance from Olivia, Gabe and Darius.

Gabe had never felt so tired. He now had new respect for catering staff. Olivia was slumped in her chair, too. She looked adorable and had worked like a demon. They all had. Winston was ecstatic. He was walking around and singing off-key, wiping tables and collecting the last few plates as he passed by.

Gabe was hoping he wasn't going to have to be the one to tell him that his 'famous' recipe had been modified. He'd leave that to Olivia.

His body protested as he tried to move. Every muscle ached, especially his leg, and he paused for a moment in pain. Olivia looked at him alarm, but he gritted his teeth and stood up. 'I think we should go home. Winston has it all covered now. Darius, where do you live? Do you need a lift home?' He asked graciously.

'I might stay over at Libby's, if that's okay?'

Olivia closed her eyes and her shoulders sunk even further into her chair. 'I have work tomorrow,' she said. 'If you don't mind sleeping on the couch and me stepping over you, that's fine. What about you, Gabe?' She held her breath about having both men stay around, but he put her out of her misery.

'It's not far from me to drive home. I parked outside.'

'I'm sorry. This wasn't the date you had planned,' said Olivia quietly, her mouth drooping.

He smiled into her eyes. 'It was fun.' He reached out and shook Winston's hand and reluctantly walked to his car. He was actually bone tired and even a kiss from Olivia couldn't keep him from his bed. He tried to ignore the pain in his leg. When he reached his car, he turned to see Olivia saying goodnight to Winston. Darius then put his arm around her and led her out onto the street. Biting back the sudden clenching of his stomach, Gabe started the engine and headed for home.

CHAPTER TWENTY-TWO

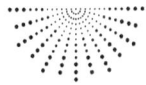

*G*abe rubbed the tiredness from his eyes and stared at the pile of paperwork on his desk. He felt like he hadn't slept for a week. He was actually considering going back to the Jacuzzi at the sports centre one night to take the edge off the pain left after his hot date – serving steaming bowls of chilli. Thank the Lord that no one from work had wandered past and seen him in the apron he'd slung around his waist to stop food splashing on his jeans.

He flipped through the files and his eyes scanned the list of women's names and details from the shelter that Darius's mum ran. He wasn't surprised to see some of them connected to the case he was working on.

He pictured Olivia's smiling face and rosy cheeks as she looked proudly at the women sitting around the tables at Winston's café the night before. Did she have the skills to make the men pay for what they had done to these women? Possibly. Probably. He tried never to underestimate his opponents, but his view was clouded by the fact that he liked Olivia. She seemed sweet and shy at times, but sometimes the way her eyes pierced his like lasers made him feel as if she could see into his soul and knew exactly what he was up to.

He shook his head to try and clear it. She'd told him that she felt invisible. Was this her way of making the world pay, and getting back at people for hurting her friends, or did she want to punish the world for ignoring her? Although why she thought it did, he couldn't fathom. As far as he could see, both men and women looked her way. She had a buzzing energy around her. He had tried not to let his feelings get in the way, but for the first time, it was difficult.

He'd also chatted to some of the women from the shelter, and he could feel their pain. They had been taught to be open and frank about their feelings, and he'd been astounded by their warmth and bravery. He felt protective of them now, dammit.

Then there was Darius. He seemed a more likely candidate... then Gabe kicked himself for being stupid. It could be either of them but, whichever it was, his gut told him he'd hit a homerun and found his hacker.

The problem was that this particular hacker could be pretty useful to him as an undercover detective in the police, in bringing down some of these men properly, as a bit of digging had revealed some pretty shady past dealings by the Damsel hacker's targets. He looked at his own damaged leg and winced at the thought of history repeating itself. He'd been shot after blurring ethical lines at work.

If Gabe could arrest one or two of these high-profile people, then he would be out of the bloody annoying open plan office and back into his old sanctuary, a side room with a view of the car park. He liked his old office because, although it was small and functional, he could see absolutely everyone who entered and left the building. He could collar anyone he needed to talk to, and avoid others by whizzing down the corridor. In the central office, he had people banging on at him the whole time about their own lives and trying to make small talk, which made his ears hum. Why the hell would he want to know what they ate for dinner the night before, or how well their child had done at school? Did he look like a family man? He did have mates and he cared about them and their families, but most of the time he enjoyed his solitary life. Work was his world. For the first time, though, he wondered if he was missing something. He hadn't grown up surrounded by loads of people, and had got used to a solitary existence when his nan had moved into the nursing home. He had never felt the need to fill his life up with people before.

He slumped over his desk for a moment, before rousing himself. He tried to rub an ache from his neck, but gave up after a minute. Suddenly adrenaline was coursing through his veins. He had the rush he usually felt when he was near to cracking a case. But were these two working alone, or were they a team? This could be why Darius was so territorial about Olivia. Perhaps she was a valuable asset?

His brain ached from trying to figure it out. Darius was friendly to Gabe, but with an edge. He smiled, but it didn't reach his eyes and Gabe didn't quite understand his intentions. Gabe sensed that Darius was either an old lover who wanted to get back together with Olivia, or a brother figure who was looking out for her now her father had passed. From the way Darius slid his hands round Olivia's waist, Gabe thought it was probably the former, but then he'd back off and flirt with Connie the same way, so Gabe was a little confused. It annoyed the hell out of him. He could usually work someone out within seconds of meeting them. Both Olivia and Darius were mysteries and he hated that.

Maybe he'd met someone who was smarter than him for the first time, but he didn't think so. Darius was cocky and would make a mistake sooner or later. Olivia, on the other hand, was sweet and pliable in his arms. His brain was foggy when he was near her. He hadn't wanted a woman this way for a long while. She enchanted him. She was unassuming, sexy and mysterious – but possibly a con artist. Perhaps she made a habit of enslaving men like him and bending them to her will.

It was making his brain ache and he needed to go and find coffee. Not the mind-blowing kind Winston made, but a soothing blend he could wash down easily while he refocused his brain on making solid links between Darius and the women at the shelter. When he was thinking clearly again, he'd find a way.

The problem was that, whatever the relationship between Darius and Olivia, she'd hate Gabe for arresting her best friend. He'd lose out either way – unless he could make her see that what they could potentially have was worth way more than being close to a criminal. Darius would let her down, or get caught one day. Worse, he could embroil her in his dealings, and then she might be at risk too. Gabe wasn't about to let that happen. He'd discover Darius's secrets, whatever the cost to his own love life. If it meant Olivia ended up free of Darius, that would be a bonus. The problem was, did she want to be free from him?

CHAPTER TWENTY-THREE

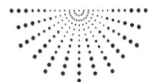

Olivia had pretty much isolated herself from everyone, when her dad had been ill. She'd known she was doing it, but had been too tired to care. Darius had always shown her kindness, though.

She slumped down onto the sofa in the big house and the dogs jumped straight on top of her, making her say 'oof'. Her back ached from carrying so many plates at the café. Waitressing was hard work. She pushed Bertie off her shoulder. He was trying to lick her face, which was disgusting.

She thought how easy it ought to be to love Darius – other than the fact that he was a criminal, of course. That was a slight flaw in the plan. She did love him, in one way, but she was also tired of cleaning up his mess. He broke hearts without meaning to. He was more like both his parents than he realised. Neither had been there for him and he was still trying to make them see him.

Olivia wasn't sure how proud his mum would be that he made his money by skimming funds from the boyfriends and husbands of the women in the shelter. However much Darius hated them, Joan would look at him with disappointment –

and would probably blame his dad, which would be wrong of her. It was her abandonment of him that had hit the hardest. He now understood she had been fighting for her life, but then she'd grown stronger, stayed local and still not reclaimed her son. She'd dedicated her life to others instead. Olivia knew Darius felt that she'd forgotten about him. It was what drove him to succeed. He wanted to show his mother what he had become, despite her.

Olivia laid her face on Belle's soft fur. The dogs had calmed down a lot since she'd been playing with them, but now that they always cried when she left it almost broke her heart in two. It made her wish she had a dog of her own. She'd started staying at the house longer and snooping around a bit, but the owners still never appeared. They left cash on the kitchen counter and a hand-written list of instructions of what to do with the dogs, which no longer involved dressing them up. The dogs loved the less ridiculous games, though, so she complied. There were no more assault courses, just indoor ball games. There was food in the fridge that got eaten, but the owners must have the appetite of sparrows. It wouldn't have lasted Olivia more than an hour, if she'd ever dared to tuck in.

Olivia sighed and got up to start cleaning the pristine kitchen again. She gave it a cursory wipe and then threw the cloth in the sink, not bothering to tidy it away. She was feeling rebellious.

One of the problems with Darius and Joan was that Joan wasn't materialistic. She practically abhorred it in others. She did accept the money Darius gave her to keep the shelter open and float her cottage industry of jam making, no real questions asked, but that made Olivia's blood boil too. If Joan gave him some praise, perhaps he'd stop trying to impress her, and go out and get a regular job. Olivia knew he could make a fortune, like she had, but he'd never taken the time to get formal qualifications or to go deeper into the technical world. He had always been the same. He had a brilliant mind, but couldn't be bothered to use it. Olivia was forever telling him to be more careful, but he laughed it off and said he was too clever to get caught.

His behaviour with Connie, made Olivia's mind whiz around in circles. He flirted with her, but there was an edge to his teasing, which was new for his relationships with women. They fell in love with his easy charm, even when he was emotionally distant. Olivia winced. His girlfriends simpered and swooned over him. Olivia knew she could be one of these women, but their friendship was too precious for her to want to risk messing with it.

She picked at her nail and then yelped when it hurt and stuck her finger in her mouth to ease the pain. Darius definitely had a soft spot for Connie, now. He'd looked out for her at the café when she was in distress. Unfortunately, that put Greg in the firing line for upsetting her. But anything Darius might do to embarrass Greg or his company would affect Connie. Olivia needed to sit down with Darius and have a serious talk. The problem was he'd still been snoring on her couch that morning, his long legs spread out onto the floor. She'd given him a kiss on the cheek. His blanket had slid off, so she'd covered him back up. He hadn't woken and she'd tiptoed out and let him sleep. He was a night owl and could easily snooze round the clock if Olivia didn't ring him to check he wasn't wasting his whole day in bed. Given a chance he'd be in her bed anyway. He'd literally drive her nuts.

But he had a posh penthouse of his own with loads of staff, and he'd soon go stir crazy in her little flat. In fact, she was starting to feel a bit claustrophobic there herself. He'd asked her to move in with him after her dad had died, but he'd demand her attention twenty-four hours a day and drive her away. He was one of those people who cleaned an already clean surface, or he had done, before he had staff to do it for him. He was slightly slobbier at her house. She grit her teeth in frustration.

She opened a cupboard and straightened a line of unopened herbs and spices, then messed them up again in annoyance, glancing over at the minimal furniture in the kitchen. She'd had a new sofa of her own, dropped off at the crack of dawn, which she'd asked the delivery people to put in her garage. She never bothered to park her car in there, as the door was quite creaky with rust. She'd also been sent some beautiful clothes, for free! Her new business idea was genius, but she was keeping it from her friends, for now.

She ran her sore finger under the tap and the cool water eased the pain. She grinned suddenly and turned the taps off, shaking her hand dry. She felt the buzz of people wanting her services again and didn't know why she had under-utilised her talents for so long. She'd never thought of bartering her time for stuff before. It worked like a dream. People wanted her services, so she said she couldn't help them until her flat and wardrobe were sorted out, as she'd donated everything when her dad died. Suddenly gifts had started arriving. Her neighbour, Mr Benson, probably thought she'd bagged a rich boyfriend, but it was all her own growing confidence in the value of her talents. It was as though a butterfly's wings were unfurling and shaking free of the chrysalis she'd built around herself. She would fully step back into her own world when she was good and ready, but if customers wanted to hurry her along by making her life more comfortable and to help with her grieving process, then so be it. She knew them all well but wasn't going to work exclusively for any of them. They'd wined and dined her before, but never sent incentives. Now word must have got round that she was deciding which clients to work with first.

Before she'd left her flat to visit the dogs that morning, she'd grabbed a box containing a pair of designer sunglasses and taken them out, marvelling at the craftsmanship. They'd arrived with an offer of a short cruise. She'd pushed them on top of her head, as the sun had been starting to show its face, and walked jauntily to her car, waving to the young couple who lived upstairs. They had frowned and seemed to be trying to remember who she was, which would have upset her a few months ago, now she couldn't have cared less.

She gave a secret smile. Her life was starting to turn round. She had two men interested in her, a new best friend, a boss who needed to keep her onside, lest she let slip to his wife that Jen hadn't been moved to another office, and at least one job she quite enjoyed. She knew she'd have to leave the relative comfort of the stationery cupboard soon as she was starting to get fidgety, but she had work she needed to do for the company first. She really did hope that Greg had changed his ways. She hadn't seen him speak directly to Jen or flirt with anyone for ages. She'd rung Connie to see if she was hungover from the night before, but she hadn't picked up, which was strange. Connie usually texted Olivia several times a day. Although she often wanted to ask about Greg, she now had frequent questions creeping in about Darius. Olivia wanted to make sure the stationery and *everything else* in the company was running smoothly before she left.

She was enjoying feeling useful to Connie. It gave her a sense of purpose. She did need to make more time for some of her old clients, and a few new ones, though. She'd put feelers out suggesting she might be ready for work again, and the requests had gratifyingly flooded in. It seemed they had all missed her, and hadn't been able to find anyone else with the same skill set. She was in demand again, and not just as a computer expert. A few new career ideas had popped into her head lately and she hadn't been able to stop thinking about them.

She glanced at the dogs, who were getting restless and sticking their noses under her hand to regain her attention. She ruffled their fur and straightened her new pink top, pulling up her jeans, noticing that they actually lovingly caressed her shape now, rather than cutting into it. She'd obviously got fitter from all the doggy dancing and playing she was doing. Clicking her fingers to switch the music system on, she began singing to the dogs, and then danced round and round with them for a good ten minutes, before they all collapsed into an exhausted heap. She was laughing loudly and it felt good to hear that sound again. She'd forgotten how much she used to laugh with her dad when he was well.

She felt tears scratch her eyes but she blinked them back. The little red light flashed silently in the corner and she hugged the dogs to her as she opened the back door to let them out. She drew in a deep breath, facing the window and looking out across the manicured lawn. If this was her house, she'd have a huge home office in the garden. One of those log cabins that looked like they'd been picked up from the mountains. Then the dogs could sit by her feet while she worked and she could get away from the rest of the house, which was a bit clinical for her taste. It could be stunning, but it needed texture and colour to soften the hard edges. She wasn't supposed to go outside with the dogs as that was her cleaning time, but she could imagine playing with them on the soft grass.

She had a plan today, though, while the dogs were busy. She was determined to get inside that third floor door. She'd even brought some tweezers from home, to try and pick the lock. But after about ten minutes of trying, she realised she'd make a rubbish burglar, as she couldn't get in.

She'd just given up and had been looking for some fresh cleaning materials under the first floor bathroom sink instead, when she'd found a key hidden in a little gilt box. The owner had obviously put it there. Maybe they didn't realise normal people used those cupboards for sponges and sprays, as there was nothing else there.

Olivia's heartbeat ramped up a notch when she saw the key and she glanced around to check if anyone was watching her, which was ridiculous. No one was ever home. She thought it would be too good to be true if it was the right key, as the top room was on the third floor and the owner probably wouldn't bother to keep taking the key up and down the stairs to hide. But she had to try. She wiped her damp brow, paused for a moment to steady her nerves and padded back upstairs to the third floor.

Sliding the key into the lock she took a huge breath as she turned it – and the door opened. She clutched onto it so that it didn't swing, but it was heavy. A wall of heat and an unusual smell hit her nostrils. She blinked as it made her eyes water and she let the door go and stood with her mouth hanging open, before snapping it shut.

She took in the rows and rows of plants and heating lamps overhead. It looked very high tech and expensive. Her eyes zeroed in on the shape of the leaves and she gasped and quickly rushed to shut the door and replace the key in its hiding place. .

What the hell? She'd read about cannabis farms, but in an exclusive abode with posh dogs and a cleaner? Now she understood why the house was so hot. She tried to slow her breathing and think clearly. Lots of pictures in her mind slotted into place and her skin flushed red. If she was found in a place like this she could be thought of as an accessory, or worse. She'd heard about lightbulb moments when everything suddenly made sense, and this was definitely one.

She wanted to scream and stamp her feet at the unfairness of it. She rushed back down to the dogs and let them in from the garden. Then her mouth set in a thin line. Enough! If this whole charade was something to do with her ex-boyfriend, then she'd tell everyone his secrets and be done with it. If he thought he could control her this way, by setting her up, luring her into the house to work with the dogs and making her an accessory to his crimes, she would make it *very* clear he was misguided. She was fed up with everyone thinking they could treat her like a doormat. They'd learn soon enough not to underestimate her.

She stomped back into the kitchen and eyed the little flashing light under the kitchen cabinet and, before she was even sure if it was the right thing to do, she picked up the phone and called one of her old contacts.

CHAPTER TWENTY-FOUR

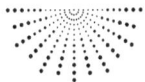

*G*abe thought Olivia looked stunning. Her hair smelt divine and her eyes were twinkling. She'd been laughing at his jokes and her hand was on his knee. They'd had a delicious Italian meal together and then moved on to a bar down the road. Nothing fancy, but they'd perched their backsides on two tall stools to the side of the bar and Gabe had given a running commentary on everyone who walked through the door. She'd asked more about his work, but he'd brushed it aside and briefly said he was a project manager for a big firm in town, which was partially true. There weren't many organisations as big as the Police.

'I'm glad you agreed to join me for dinner.' He scooped her hair over her shoulder and her skin flushed at his touch, but her eyes never left his. 'How was Connie after the night at Winston's café?'

Olivia ran her hand along his thigh and his words trailed off as he focused on where her hand was travelling. 'I haven't heard from her, other than one text to say she's decided to leave Greg. I've tried calling but she won't pick up.'

He caught her hand before it went too near his groin and

pressed it to his lips, his eyes sparkling. He was trying to gauge her mood. She'd been very attentive all night and he was really enjoying himself. He wanted to throw her over his shoulder and carry her to bed, but didn't want to scare her away. She didn't seem anything but happy tonight. He ran his hand up her thigh in turn and she inhaled sharply and caught his hand too, slipping it behind her waist and leaning in for a searing kiss that almost knocked him off his chair. He was so hot afterwards he licked his lips, wanting more. His eyes dilated and he leaned in for another, but she just pressed a quick kiss to his lips and sipped her drink, so he had to sit back. He kept hold of her waist, slipping his hand down to her derriere and making her giggle into her drink.

'I thought Connie would stay with him forever, she seemed so devoted,' he said when he'd regained his composure and could think straight. They had started speaking to each other on the phone every night and he'd enjoyed hearing about her life and friends. She still kept him at arm's length when he asked about Darius, though.

She wriggled so she was touching knees with him and put her hands on his legs. He was glad that his wound was finally starting to heal properly and he didn't flinch.

'I thought so too,' Olivia said. 'But she's a lot more aware of what he's doing now. She's watching his every move. Going away for the weekend was a stupid mistake, although when I went into work the next day, it seems he really had been at a conference and did meet clients. But his old personal assistant, Jen, was booked in as well.' She didn't mention how she knew this information and he assumed it must be office gossip.

Olivia rolled her eyes at Greg's antics and sat back to take another sip of her Mojito, sighing in bliss and giving Gabe a chance to admire her neck. He really wanted to bite and lick his way up and down her body.

This was getting ridiculous! He tried to recall the last time he'd got laid, or even really been interested, but the way he was feeling about Olivia was more than that. He thought about her all the time.

Things were getting messy. His bosses had dropped the cannabis case as a hoax and his phishing Damsel hacker friend was busy setting up more men who had hurt others, so the incident count was growing. It seemed like the hacker was getting angrier, and taking on more than one person at a time now. Before, it had been one or two every so often. Now incidents were cropping up all the time. There were solid links to the shelter where Darius and Olivia helped out. With her background, it made sense.

He was holding back, though, as he still hadn't been honest about what his job was yet. He needed to look her in the eye when he told her, but was worried what she'd say. He would know if it was her or Darius who was involved, by her reaction to the news. He shuffled uncomfortably in his seat. The problem was, he'd risk her hating him for lying. He felt her hand slide up his thigh to capture his attention again. 'Sorry,' he smiled, sipping his cold beer. 'The man's an idiot for treating Connie that way.'

'He is,' sighed Olivia, removing her hand and sitting straighter. 'He's too used to getting everything he wants and he should watch out in case he gets burnt.'

Gabe's eyes went wide and he spluttered on his drink, so she patted him on the back, affording a glorious view of her chest. He tried to stay focused. 'How could he get burnt? I thought she didn't have anything conclusive on him?'

Olivia's eyes had been glazed for a second, but now she wrinkled her nose and reached for her drink. He noticed it was almost empty and signalled to the waitress for another. 'There are ways of finding out what he's up to,' she said.

'Really? How?' He felt his heartbeat ramp up a notch and his palms began to sweat.

She paused for a fraction and looked around the bar. 'Connie said she set a private investigator on him before, but she could look into his purchase history and phone records... I guess.'

'Isn't that illegal?'

'Is it? I don't know. I'm not an expert, but he's probably got paper copies of his phone bill or keeps them online on his computer. He might have receipts stored, if he's organised.'

'Ah. I thought you meant someone could hack him?' He stared straight at her but she threw back her head and laughed.

'What do you know about hacking? Are you a computer expert?' She giggled and he couldn't help but smile back, though there was an uneasy feeling in his stomach.

'Not at all.' He drew in a breath. 'I did read somewhere about people who had been hacked and had large sums of money stolen, though. That must be awful for them. It seems like it's been happening with various victims for years, but this hacker has been elusive – until recently. Perhaps he's getting old, or sloppy.'

Olivia stopped smiling. 'I hadn't read about that. Was it in a local paper?'

He faltered. Oh man! What paper could the article have been in? Probably all of them. 'I think it was a local paper somewhere. I saw it when I went out of the city last week. Some shady rich people had their bank accounts drained.'

'Really? That sounds awful! Why would someone do that?'

That's what we're trying to work out, he said to himself. 'Vengeance, it seems, or that's what it said in the article. A modern day Robin Hood.'

'It said that?'

'Ah… no. That's just my thoughts on the matter.'

'You think they're doing the right thing, then?'

'They?'

She kept her eyes on him and sipped her fresh drink steadily. 'You said 'him,' but it could be a woman or a group, couldn't it? Or the person who was wronged in the first place?'

'The hacker steals money from the victim and probably treats himself – or herself – with it.' He eyed her sexy new, expensive-looking top, and the jeans that skimmed her figure and complemented her eyes.

'I thought you said they gave it to the poor?'

'That's just a theory.'

'You've obviously thought about it a lot.'

'Not really. The topic just caught my eye and it was a boringly long journey. What do you think about it?'

'I think you need another beer, and we should get out of here and go dancing.'

He gulped. 'Dancing? Have you seen the state of my leg?'

Gabe let the subject go for now, but he knew he'd have to talk to her about it, before someone else from the station did. The amount of information he'd requested about the Damsel hacker was now substantial. He'd have to show some results to his bosses soon. He needed to reveal what he'd found about her connection to the women's shelter and the case, or quickly find some sort of resolution for the victims, or the targets, as he still thought of them.

The whole situation was getting complicated and he wished he'd never set eyes on the damn case in the first place.

CHAPTER TWENTY-FIVE

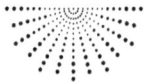

*O*livia yawned and stretched in her brand new double bed. It was so plush and comfortable that she could easily have slept for days. She'd agreed to terms for two new clients and fitted them in between everything else going on in her life. Her days were getting busier. The downside was she didn't have a lot of time for Gabe, Darius or Connie.

Gabe had stayed over a few times now. He'd taken her dancing, despite his leg, and they had fallen into an exhausted heap on her bed, before she was woken up in the early hours of the next day by his hands trailing lazily across her skin, sending arrows of fire as his fingers crept down from her waist, across her thighs. She'd turned to face him and he'd had a question in his eyes. She'd answered him by leaning in and capturing his lips, making him groan and start kissing his way down her body until she lost complete sense of her mind and gave herself up to the moment.

When he'd finally pressed his body into hers, she was glad he had brought protection and she gently bit into his shoulder as he sighed her name.

He set her skin on fire with his touch and she was loath to

let him go when he had to get up for work hours later. She couldn't keep the smug grin off her face and he'd waltzed naked into the shower, making her eyes water at the sight of his beautiful body, firm muscles glistening and taut. He'd put out a hand for her to join him and she hadn't needed asking twice. He'd reluctantly left for work with a promise to come back later, which made her grin and blush at the same time.

After he'd made her a quick coffee, she'd noticed that he'd taken an interest in her flat and had commented on her new furnishings. She'd sipped her drink and admitted that she had a third job which was actually very productive and allowed her to work from home. He'd asked her about it and she'd joked that she was a master criminal and she conned people into sending her free stuff. He'd looked shocked and then laughed and picked her up and carried her back to bed, where he'd kissed her again until she was panting his name and then pulled himself away, tucking her hair behind her ear and leaving for work before he was tempted to strip off again, which she wouldn't have minded at all.

Now the doorbell rang and she yawned and slipped her feet into designer slippers and pulled on a silk robe and tied it around her waist. Running her fingers through her now permanently glossy hair, she peeked into the new updated video intercom and grinned when she saw Gabe standing there, looking restless and sexy.

She pressed the buzzer to let him in and he said a polite hello to Mr Benson who was craning his neck from the next floor bannister, to see who her guest was. He harrumphed loudly and ignored Gabe, which made them both smile as he came inside. 'I thought you had work today?'

'That was yesterday.' He rolled his eyes with good humour. 'I'm so glad our conversations are memorable. It's the weekend.'

She frowned. All her days were blending into one at the

moment. Then she pulled him back into her little bedroom and onto the squishy bed, which almost filled the room from wall to wall. It clashed with the old brown wardrobe. This had a wonky door where she'd slammed into it while kissing Gabe and trying to manoeuvre around the bed one night. She always grinned at the memory, so the broken door was staying.

Gabe pinned her to the bed so that her arms were above her head and she drew in a breath as he kissed her. Then he looked into her eyes. 'I came round to invite you to breakfast by the sea.'

She licked her lips, her eyes shining. 'It's the weekend. They serve breakfast all day by the sea.' She pulled him so that their bodies were in closer contact and wrapped her legs around him, making him dip down and capture her lips. She ran her fingers through his thick hair and a moan escaped her, just as the buzzer went on her front door and they both froze.

Gabe rolled sideways and Olivia bit her lip, listening out to see if the person at the door would go away. The incessant buzzing grew louder.

'Another delivery?' he joked.

Olivia swung her legs off the side of the bed and winced when she looked into the intercom video and saw Darius standing outside, his face pinched and eyes bloodshot. She frowned and buzzed him in without thinking, then remembered he'd left his spare key in the kitchen one night and she hadn't returned it yet. He came in straight away and pushed past her, as if he had something urgent to say. He stopped suddenly when he saw Gabe in her bed and blanched, turning to Olivia.

'I thought you might be ill, as I hardly hear from you these days? Obviously you've found someone else to fill your time.'

Olivia looked from a very smiley and relaxed Gabe, who waved genially, to a twitchy Darius. She led Darius into the kitchen and turned the kettle on, noticing the door key and quickly sliding it under the toaster. 'Gabe came round to invite me for breakfast.'

'In your bedroom?'

'I'm a grown woman, Darius.'

He looked at her glossy hair and silky dressing gown up and down in contempt. 'I can see that. You've got new furniture. How have you afforded that? Did he buy it? Is he moving in?' Darius flicked his head towards her bedroom.

'No. Of course he didn't, and no, he isn't.' She sighed and gave him a disapproving stare, handing him a steaming coffee. 'I've decided to take on some work again.'

Darius's whole demeanour changed. He put down the coffee and then swung her up and around the tiny kitchen, almost whacking her legs on the counter top. 'That's amazing! I knew you'd see the light. Who are you working for?'

Gabe walked into the kitchen and Olivia wriggled so that Darius very slowly put her down. She turned her back to Gabe for a second and gave Darius a warning look.

Darius grinned and kissed her on the lips. 'I'm thrilled to hear your happy news.' He looked at Gabe, who was frowning and about to say something, but interrupted him. 'Looks like you two are busy, so I'll leave you to your *breakfast*. I can't wait for us to be back working together again soon.' He swept out of the kitchen and left the flat, leaving Gabe waiting for answers and Olivia furious over his childish games.

'You work together?'

She sipped her coffee and waited for her insides to stop churning. Darius was such an idiot. He had no right to kiss her in front of Gabe.

'I'm so sorry about his behaviour. He thinks he owns me.'

Gabe put his coffee down and stood before her, looking into her eyes. 'Why does he think that?'

She tried not to shake and leaned on the kitchen counter for support. 'We're the only family each other has, really.'

'He doesn't treat you like family,' he said carefully, clearly trying to control his temper.

'We used to work together a long time ago and he's been trying to persuade me to go back for ages. I like working on my own projects. He's a bit bossy,' she tried to joke, pulling the cord of her robe tighter around her waist. 'He's very territorial and doesn't think anyone is good enough for me.'

'Because he wants you for himself,' stated Gabe. Her skin grew warm and she couldn't look up into his eyes.

'I don't feel the same way about him though. I love him – just not like that.'

'Maybe you should make that clear?' he ground out, handing her the coffee and lifting her face to look at him.

'I've tried, but he's stubborn and won't listen. He's used to getting anything he wants.' She wandered into the lounge and sank onto the couch. He followed her, but stayed standing.

'Maybe it's time he learnt some boundaries.'

She bit her bottom lip and he then sat on the couch next to her and pulled her onto his lap.

'What did you used to do together, work wise?'

'We designed computer programmes for clients. To streamline their businesses and safeguard them.' He didn't look as shocked as she'd expected. 'We haven't worked as a team for a while and he wants us back together.'

'In more ways than one, it seems?' She cringed and hid her face in his shoulder. His arms were still around her, but they weren't quite as comforting as usual. She pushed softly against the solid wall of his chest and unfurled her legs, standing up and looking down at him. He really was gorgeous, but then so was Darius. At least Gabe wasn't trying to rule her life and influence her decisions… or was he?

CHAPTER TWENTY-SIX

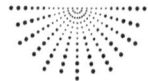

*O*livia rubbed her tired eyes and looked through her wardrobe for something to wear. She chose a soft skirt that swished around her legs, as the weather was starting to warm up, and pulled on a lightly patterned jumper in a complementing colour. She shut the door behind her and walked out of the flat. Darius's jealousy was getting worse. She'd tried to talk to him and be very clear what their relationship was, but he was sulking. She couldn't bear not to have him in her life, so she was walking a fine line.

Her conversations with Connie were strained, too. It was why all three of them were meeting at Winston's café. Olivia felt the adrenaline flow around her body and wondered why she was shaking. She wasn't sure what had gone wrong, other than Gabe entering the picture, of course. Olivia wasn't at Connie's beck and call as much now, either. But she wanted them all to be friends again.

Darius barely looked up when she walked in. He was standing there in jeans and a dove grey shirt rolled up to his elbows, leaning on the counter. He was chatting to Winston, who was throwing his head back and laughing at something Darius had said. Olivia couldn't help but smile. Darius could charm honey from bees. She walked over to them and Winston made a huge fuss of her and brought her favourite coffee, settling them both at a table by the back of the fairly busy shop.

'Have you heard from Connie?' Olivia tucked her little sky blue handbag by her feet and crossed her legs, looking into Darius's face. His eyes narrowed for a fraction of a second and then he looked away. 'You didn't sleep with her? Oh Darius! Why the hell did you do that?'

He lifted his face and looked at her and she winced. 'You were all loved up and I wanted some company.'

She rolled her eyes, before facing him again, her skin feeling warm. 'You did it to wind me up?"

It was his turn to flush this time, but he didn't turn away. 'She's filed for divorce from Greg.'

'What?'

He gave her a smug look and she could have wiped it off his face. 'Are you committed to her?' When he looked confused she kicked him and he yelped. 'She's leaving him for you, you idiot!'

'What? No, she isn't. We've just slept together a couple of times. We were both missing you.'

'So you comforted her by having sex with her?'

He spluttered out the coffee he had just begun to drink, just as Connie came through the door and gazed around to find them. Her eyes lit up when she saw Darius and she even sent a smile to Olivia. She scooched in next to him and turned her face for a kiss. Olivia sent him a pointed glare and he jumped up to get Connie a coffee.

'How are you?' asked Olivia. 'I haven't heard from you much.'

Connie's eyes were following Darius, but she turned back to face Olivia. 'Sorry. I was a bit jealous about the whole Gabe situation, but it made me see that perhaps I could find a hunky guy if I was single. If you can do it, anyone can.'

'Um, thanks... I think.'

'I've asked Greg to move out, but he won't go. I've told him about Darius and he's raging. He wants to face Darius and tell him to leave me alone.'

'Isn't that what you wanted, for Greg to notice you?' asked Olivia gently. 'Are you and Darius a thing?'

Connie looked round. 'Are you ok with that?' She reached for Olivia's hand. 'I wouldn't want to do anything to upset you and I know he's like a brother to you. We could almost all be family now!'

Olivia's jaw dropped. She tried to analyse her feelings. She did want everyone to be happy, however weird the situation. 'Um, sure. Of course. Have you spoken to Darius about how he feels?'

Connie winked and stared at his backside again. 'He's shown me plenty enough. He can't keep his hands off me. Greg wants to kill him,' she smiled smugly. 'It's nice to be in control for a change.'

Olivia looked at Connie's immaculate blond hair, made-up face and designer outfit and smiled suddenly. 'You certainly look good together. I've missed you.'

Connie preened and sat a bit taller as Darius returned with fresh coffees for them all, and slices of chocolate cake for the ladies. He sat next to Connie again and she linked arms with him, which made him look uncomfortable suddenly.

Olivia took a huge bite of cake and sighed in bliss. 'Who needs men when you have cake?'

Connie burst out laughing and Olivia handed Darius a

fork so that he could share her cake. He took a huge mouthful and he almost went crossed-eyed with pleasure. It was like old times, and they bent their heads together and planned a night out, that might or might not include Gabe.

CHAPTER TWENTY-SEVEN

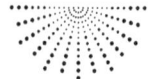

*G*reg ran his hands through his hair and succeeded in making it stand on end. Olivia tried to avoid him but he marched toward her and practically dragged her into his office. He pulled out a chair for her and then strode to his own seat.

'I guess you want to speak to me, Greg?' she tried to joke, but he stared at her, before getting up and pacing the room, making her head spin.

'You have to help me, Olivia. She'll listen to you.'

'Who will?' She looked at the people buzzing around outside, going about their daily business or indulging in the usual office gossip. Being in Greg's room with the door closed was enough to set tongues wagging, Olivia knew that. People had started to talk to her now that she wasn't always staring at the floor, and she had made a few casual friends, including the new girl.

Greg stopped pacing and looked at her as if she was thick. 'Connie, of course! She's asked for a divorce.'

Olivia edged out of her seat and wondered if she could make a run for it, but he stood in front of her, his usually pristine grey suit creased, with a coffee stain in an unfortunate place. Now that she'd seen it, she couldn't take her eyes off it. She finally raised her face to his and put on a sympathetic expression. 'Ah… yes. I had heard that. I'm not sure what help I could be.'

'She told me you introduced her to this Darius?' he ground out and she felt like he wanted to scream at her for that, but was just about holding his cool.

'I suppose I did. He's my best friend.'

'What sort of friend hits on your girlfriends?'

She gave him a look and he backed off and slumped into his seat again, his head in his hands. Jen walked past the door and gazed in and Olivia gave her a tight smile.

'Why Jen?' Olivia asked Greg.

He seemed as if he was going to deny it, but then rubbed the back of his neck and sat back in his seat, watching her.

'I love Connie and I've made a huge mistake. Jen meant nothing.' He saw her disgust and flinched. 'Connie's obsessed by her parents and this bloody company. She keeps coming up with ideas that don't work and pushes for me to share them, which makes it awkward for me and her parents.' He slurped from the mug of cold tea on his desk and then wrinkled his nose in disgust. 'Things have grown strained,' he implored her to understand. 'I felt I couldn't live up to her expectations or her parents' standards for me, so in the end I gave up. Whatever I do, it's not good enough for her. She thinks she's developing the company and I just front it for her. I've been fighting fires between her and her parents for years and it's exhausting. They are all control freaks.'

'So you acted out?'

He flushed and started playing with the pens from the pot in front of him. He saw the sparkly gold one that Jen had left there and threw it into the bin by his feet. 'I didn't think she'd care, from the amount of attention she shows me. She likes it when I'm showering her with gifts or compliments, but otherwise I might as well be dead.'

Olivia could feel her stomach churning. She didn't want to be stuck between these two. Connie was her friend, but Greg was just her soon-to-be ex-boss. She did want them both to be happy, but perhaps they'd be better off without each other?

'I need you to talk to her for me. Please?'

She stood up and threw her hands in the air. 'Oh, for goodness sake, Greg! You did this. You need to sort it out,' she said as she walked out and then shut the door firmly behind her. She gave Jen a fake smile and marched over to the stationery cupboard to steal some pens to use in the new home office she was determined to set up soon. Then she opened up the computer and typed out her notice.

CHAPTER TWENTY-EIGHT

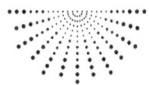

Olivia stared in awe at the front of Connie and Greg's house. It really was astounding. It was a mere twenty-minute drive from her flat, but it was the biggest house she'd ever seen, except for the palace the Royal Family lived in, of course. She had been expecting something historical and magnificent, but this building was streamlined and modern. It had floor-to-ceiling windows and lots of steel and beams. It was like something out of a design magazine. She parked her car and turned off the engine, trying to still her beating heart. Why had Connie suddenly invited her to her home? Perhaps now that she was chucking Greg out, she didn't care who crossed the threshold. Plus, Olivia was decidedly less frumpy and embarrassing than she had been when they'd met.

Trying to ignore the crunchy sound of the gravel underfoot, she walked up to the door, but it swung open before she could press the intercom.

Olivia knew she had to broach the 'Greg' topic, but Connie's mood was up and down all the time at the moment. She texted Olivia at all hours of the day and night for advice on how to keep Darius's attention. Olivia hadn't been able to offer much help. She'd always tried to stay well out of Darius's love life. This had infuriated Connie and made her unfairly accuse Olivia of wanting him for herself. Now there was this sudden invitation to her house.

'Libby!' Connie threw her arms round her and almost dragged her indoors.

Libby? What the hell?

'Darius is on his way over.'

'Ah,' said Olivia. *So we're friends again because of Darius. This girlfriends lark is so confusing!* She pushed down the sudden urge to run back outside, immediately.

Connie almost skipped down the cavernous entrance-way, past the all-glass staircase that must be a logistical nightmare if you were ever wearing a skirt. They walked into a huge sitting room that in turn led to a kitchen, which made Olivia stand stock still in awe. It was the most beautiful space she had ever seen, with granite surfaces, steel fittings and a huge island unit in the centre that could easily seat about twenty people. The fixtures glistened in the sunshine and she looked out through the floor-to-ceiling windows onto a lush manicured lawn and garden.

'This is absolutely stunning, Connie.'

Connie waved her hand as if to brush off the praise. Olivia supposed she was used to it. 'Take a seat.'

Reaching up on tiptoes, Connie got out three wine glasses for the bottle of red that had already been poured into a decanter and was waiting on the counter top. Olivia dreaded to think how much it cost. It wasn't one of the bottles Connie had brought round to Olivia's house, but even they had been delicious and pricey.

'Have you just moved in?' The lack of fuss or personal items gave it a sterile feel.

Connie frowned. 'We've lived here for ages. Greg chose the house,' she scoffed, as if she hated mentioning his name.

Olivia took a sip of the wine and sighed in bliss. It really was delicious. 'About that… Greg's been calling me into his office and asking me for help.'

Connie's head snapped up and her smile slipped. 'Why is he talking to you?'

Olivia raised her eyebrows over the rim of her glass and inhaled the aroma of fruit and sunshine. 'Because I'm your friend.'

Connie's eyes flashed and she stood facing Olivia on the other side of the island. 'Are you? You have two great guys and don't want either. I have one useless one and I can't get rid of him. He's refusing to move out and has taken his stuff into a spare room at the other side of the house. He's hardly ever here, though. Probably out with that strumpet.'

'He's not out. He's spending hours and hours of extra time at work.'

Connie's eyes narrowed and her mouth formed a thin line. She looked a little flustered already and slugged more wine back, making Olivia wince. She couldn't face another night like the one at Winston's.

'He's trying so hard to win you back. He might be an idiot, but is there no chance for you at all?'

'He's not worth it.'

'Really?'

'Really,' stated Connie with finality.

Olivia peered out over the big slate grey patio and beyond, to the lawn, which bordered a pool towards the back of the property with a huge summer house behind it. Olivia remembered Connie saying she had a pool house in the garden, but the building looked like a small wood-built bungalow! She could just see the glint of the water moving in the light. What she wouldn't give to be doing laps in that right now? She thought back to that first swimming date with Gabe, and his searing kisses. She'd have to deal with him as well, soon. She couldn't keep putting off the inevitable. Today, she'd decided to take control back from all of them. She squared her shoulders, took a tiny sip of wine so her head would stay clear, and chose her words carefully.

'About Greg… I need to talk to you about him.'

'I know about you and Greg!' seethed Connie. If looks could have killed, Olivia would have been stone cold dead at that moment.

Olivia looked her straight in the eye, carefully placing her delicate wine glass back onto the granite. 'I know you do.'

'What do you mean, you know I do?' said Connie angrily, as if she was talking to a stupid child.

The intercom buzzed and Connie slapped her own glass down, almost snapping the stem in two, and looked to see who it was. She blanched when she saw Darius. She didn't bother to go to the door, but just pressed the button to let him in. *He's obviously been here before then*, thought Olivia.

Connie ignored Olivia and started preening, straightening her lightweight mohair jumper and smoothing down her hair. Olivia rolled her eyes. Darius smiled at Olivia when he came in and then the grin slid from his face as he looked from woman to woman. Going straight to Olivia, he hugged her, and then turned to face Connie, which seemed to enrage her further.

Picking up her wine again, Connie sloshed more from the bottle into her now-empty glass. 'You have no idea what I'm talking about do you, you ignoramus?' she sneered at Olivia. 'You're a slut who gets off on men's slavish devotion.'

Olivia's mouth fell open and Darius went to take Connie's arm and move the wine from her grasp.

'What the hell's going on?' he asked. 'I thought we were all going out for dinner?'

'I'm not sure Olivia will want to go,' said Connie manically. 'I found out that she'd been shagging my husband, so I decided to keep her close and then post videos online of her making a fool of herself entertaining two delinquent dogs, so she could see how it felt to be made to look ridiculous.'

Darius went white. Connie waited for the explosion from them both, and turned to see why Olivia wasn't screaming at her, or smashing things. Not that there was much around to smash, other than the wine decanter and glasses.

'I know,' said Olivia calmly, sipping her wine and watching Connie. She was glad there was a huge slab of granite between them. 'I've known all along who you are and what you've done.'

Connie's face creased and she rubbed her eyes, wobbling slightly on her feet. Darius put his arm around her and led her to a tall metal stool, but she pushed him away.

'What do you know?' she rounded on Olivia, but Darius was faster and held them apart. Olivia hadn't moved from her seat at the breakfast bar. 'And how the hell *could* you know what I've done?' spat Connie.

'I saw the camera and traced it.' Olivia's hand was shaking, so she put the wine down and placed her hands in her lap.

'Don't be ridiculous! How the hell could you do that?' Connie's face was red with anger now.

Darius grinned in admiration and seemed relieved, his hand still on Connie's arm. 'It's fairly simple if you know what you're doing.'

'How the hell can a dog sitter know what she's doing?' sneered Connie, pointedly looking at Darius's hand until he dropped it to his side.

'She's not just a dog sitter,' he said carefully, helping Connie over to a window seat that was stuffed with plump orange cushions.

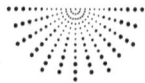

'*J*'m a dog owner,' interrupted Olivia, making them both turn round.

'What?' asked Connie.

'What?' Darius spoke at the same time. 'Neither of you are making sense.'

'I own those dogs,' said Olivia simply.

Connie scoffed and sat back, looking Olivia up and down. 'No you don't, they belong to a shelter. I borrow them to make you look stupid. Those dogs are exhausting!'

It was Olivia's turn to get angry now. Her eyes blazed, making Connie baulk. 'I love those dogs. They're just lonely. All of us should be able to relate to that! You tried to set me up, because I slept with Greg,' she accused.

Connie laughed drily. 'You deserved it.' Her face fell when she saw Darius's expression and looked at him for understanding. His face was set in stone.

'Then why pretend to be my friend?' Olivia really wanted to know.

Connie slumped down into the cushions and leaned back

on the window. 'To find out if you were still sleeping with him. I hadn't planned on Jen entering the picture. I didn't realise I'd actually start to like you either,' she answered. 'I do, but I still hate you as well.'

'You slept with *Greg*?' asked Darius, turning to face his best friend.

Olivia threw up her arms in exasperation. 'It was ages ago. Not that it's an excuse.' She looked at Connie, apologetically. 'He told me he was single. I don't know why you're pretending to be shocked,' she glared at Darius. 'You already know this information. Don't you?' she eyed him warily, her cheeks flushed red. 'We might as well air all our dirty linen.'

'What? I don't know what you mean.' Darius didn't look at her, but went to fetch a wine glass and pour some in. Finally he turned to face her.

'See!' shouted Connie. 'She's a sleaze bag.'

'I wouldn't have gone near him if I'd known he was married. He's the sleaze!' Olivia jumped down from her stool and started pacing.

'You must have known he was married. How could you not know? You work together!'

'We'd finished before I got the job. He finished it,' said Olivia. 'At the time I thought my heart was broken. Now I know I was just grieving, lonely and stupid.'

Connie stopped talking for a minute and digested this piece of information, frowning. 'He finished it? I thought he must be in love with you.'

'What? Why?'

'He gave you a job to keep you close. He's never done anything like that before.'

Olivia raised her eyes to the heavens and counted to ten. 'No, he didn't. I applied online and he was horrified when he saw me. He still didn't tell me he was married, the bastard. I found out at the Christmas party, when I met you. I was appalled. You were so kind and lovely that I wanted to make things better for you.' Olivia tried to let more air into her constricted lungs and not let anxiety take over. 'Little did I know what you are really like, posting videos of me online! Greg and I had been over for months by then. I'd have dumped his sorry arse first if I'd known.'

Connie wailed and Darius rushed over to hold her while she sobbed into his arms.

Olivia stared at her dispassionately. 'The dancing dog clips weren't humiliating enough for you though, were they Connie? You wanted me gone.' Her body ached and her head throbbed. 'You tried to set me up by buying a house in my name and filling the top floor with a cannabis factory! What the hell was *that* all about? You are completely unhinged. Who does that? No one!' Olivia's heart felt like it was beating out of her chest and her blood was boiling. 'Have you got so much money that you'll give a house away just to get revenge?'

'You have got to be joking?' said Darius, to Connie. 'Isn't that a bit extreme? You told me you thought Greg had loads of affairs.' Olivia winced and he realised his mistake, but had obviously gone beyond caring too.

'I wanted her to pay for being the first woman Greg had loved, besides me. It had to be over the top, to make her see I meant business.'

'He didn't love me, you stupid woman,' said Olivia. 'He got rid of me the minute he thought I started to like him. Sorry, Connie.' Connie's eyes were wide and wild now. Her hair was a mess and she was shaking. 'I was at an all-time low and my dad had just died,' continued Olivia. 'I'd have known he was lying if I'd have been fully *compos mentis*.'

Connie sagged in her seat, head in her hands. 'I was so sure.'

'I could have gone to prison, Connie!' Olivia was just about reigning in her temper. Underneath was a volcano that wanted to explode.

'How were you planning to get the house back?' asked Darius, looking pointedly at Connie. She didn't answer.

'She probably hadn't even thought that far ahead. She just wanted to get me into the maximum amount of trouble with her idiotic scheme. A big house like that is nothing to a millionairess. Knowing her, she thought I was so stupid that I'd just hand it back and leave in shame. All she wanted was for me to be arrested and embarrassed.' Connie gasped and hid her face.

'You can't be serious, Connie?' snapped Darius. 'Supposing they hadn't let her out?'

'She wouldn't have cared,' said Olivia simply, her anger vanishing suddenly. Her shoulders slumped and she leaned on the counter. 'She can afford a hundred houses.' Connie's silence spoke volumes.

Olivia rubbed her eyes. She stared out towards the garden again and pictured the dogs in the kitchen of the other house. 'I'm keeping the house.'

Connie jumped up. 'You can't do that!'

'I can,' said Olivia calmly. 'You tried to send me to prison for something I didn't do.'

'For goodness sake! They would probably have just fined you…'

Olivia's death stare silenced her. 'I've earned that house, through all the stupid videos you posted of me online. Did you ever actually check back and look at them?'

Connie snatched the wine from Darius and took a mouthful, ignoring him. 'No, why should I? They did their job. I made sure the first one was posted, then I forgot about them. I paid a lot of money for someone else to keep posting them for me. You are *not* keeping that house.'

'Did you check to see if you're still paying them? The house is in my name. It's my house.'

Connie scoffed, smiling at Darius, who shook his head. 'I paid for the property, so it's mine.'

Olivia laughed at last. 'Did you? You were careful to pay in cash, so who knows who bought the house? You really do have more money than sense,' she said scornfully.

Darius was incredulous and Connie stamped her feet, narrowly missing his toes.

Olivia sighed and went on. 'And you told the people at the hair salon I'd slept with Greg?' It had been days before Olivia had been able to walk straight after her waxing.

Connie grinned evilly. 'You deserved it. They barely cut your hair, painted your nails the colour of mud, and charged you a fortune for it.'

Olivia ignored her and pulled her laptop from the bag by her feet, tapping the keys until the screen sprang to life. She rested it on the kitchen counter and brought up the dancing dog videos.

'I'm not going to look.' Connie's face went white. 'I wanted you to be humiliated, but after I met you I couldn't watch.'

'You still paid a company to post them, though?' Olivia held her breath and waited.

'I couldn't let you just sleep with my husband and walk away,' said Connie, nostrils flaring. She stared at the videos and let out a howl of pain. Olivia's face was completely obscured. Then she frowned and looked at the stats on followers and rankings. Her eyes went wide with shock. 'What the hell?'

Olivia let out her breath and gave Connie a full view of the screen. 'It seems I'm not as invisible as I thought. The videos trend every time they're posted. I'm Internet famous.'

'Your face is blacked out! How did you do that?' demanded Connie. She slammed her hands onto the counter, making them all jump.

Olivia turned to Darius, raising an enquiring eyebrow. He flushed bright red.

CHAPTER THIRTY

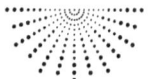

'*I* was checking you were safe by reviewing surveillance feeds at your new job and saving your dignity,' he said, pleading for understanding. 'I couldn't find who posted them, as it was rerouted millions of times. I kept telling you to leave that job. Both jobs in fact.' He ran his hands through his hair and swore under his breath. 'Working with Greg was never a good idea either. He doesn't treat women with respect.' His skin flushed as she raised her eyes to his and stayed silent. 'Plus Connie's clever! No wonder she owns a tech company.'

'Her dad owns it,' said Olivia drily. 'I re-routed the video after it was sent each time. I had control. I saw you'd doctored the first one and added the app to the feed, so I knew my face was covered. You happily left it there for the world to see, though, Darius… Why?'

'I couldn't work out who posted the video clips. I was embarrassed that I couldn't take them down.'

'I'll still report you for growing cannabis,' threatened Connie. 'Give me the house back. I took photos of the room as proof.'

'Darius has already done your dirty work for you, Connie,' said Olivia sadly. 'He was upset with me for ignoring him, I guess, or for sleeping with Greg, so he reported the cannabis factory to the police.' She closed her eyes for a moment and chose her words carefully. 'He found a ready-made scenario where he could get me away from both of you. You did him a favour,' she said sadly. 'He didn't think it through, either. I could have been arrested, you idiots!' she yelled, eyes flashing. 'Darius knew you owned the house the whole time, and he knew why you wanted to be my friend. He played us both. He's as bad as Greg. Why don't you ask him about it?'

She looked at Darius but her eyes were dull now, and her bones felt like they were filled with lead. Connie was staring at Darius with the same disgust Olivia had felt when she found out the part he'd played in this fiasco.

Olivia did have one parting shot before she left, though. 'Have you ever actually seen a cannabis plant, Connie?'

Connie faltered. 'Of course! I planted them.'

Olivia rolled her eyes. 'Did you buy the plants off of the Internet?' Connie flushed and Darius groaned and put his head in his hands as if it weighed a ton. 'Do you really think your friendly pot dealer would sell actual cannabis plants online to Joe public?'

Connie's mouth hung open. 'He delivered them to the house,' she reasoned. Darius groaned again and closed his eyes, pressing his thumbs to his temples.

'They're different plants, Connie! You've been conned, you sad, sad, woman.' Connie stared at her. 'They are almost the same, except one's legal and one's not. The leaves are almost identical, but the texture of them is completely different. The whole house would have reeked and I'd have been off my head all the time working there, with the heat upstairs.'

She gazed at her two ex-friends. 'I'm not taping you or trying to get you to confess, or even have you thrown in jail for the appalling way you've behaved.' She turned to Connie. 'Why couldn't you just cut up his clothes and ignore me, like a normal person? That would have hurt both of us enough.'

Darius shook his head and looked at Connie with pity. 'Come on, Olivia. I think I should take you home.' Olivia wanted to get out of there, even if it meant leaving with Darius. She'd deal with him later.

'Now that you've destroyed this home! My marriage is over,' Connie shouted at them.

Olivia turned and sadly replied. 'You did that all on your own.' She pushed a file onto the kitchen counter, in front of Connie.

'What's this?'

'It's what I used to do, before my dad got ill. And what I'm building a business around again now. I did a vulnerability report on your empire.'

'What the hell are you talking about?'

'Olivia runs one of the country's finest cybercrime companies,' said Darius. He was trying to stop Olivia from hating him, but in reality she'd wanted to punch his face for ages. Connie's, too. She'd bided her time, though.

'What the hell?' joked Connie. 'She can't seriously have altered the video feeds? I assume you were making that up? She works in the stationery cupboard.'

'Yet I still managed to hack in and find out all about your company from the antiquated machine in there,' said Olivia.

Connie faltered, but was listening now. 'How?'

'Whatever you say, Greg is actually an asset to your firm. He's streamlined your ideas and made them work. Before that they were just ideas. They weren't even great ideas.'

'You looked at our private development files?'

Olivia shrugged. 'Yep, and if I can, so can others... well, they could have done. Not now.'

Connie was getting angry again and her skin was growing more flushed by the minute. 'What do you mean? You're talking in riddles.'

'I mean that I'm taking the house, but I'm offering to help you out in return. Do you know your firm wastes £300 on tea each year? The staff steal £5000 worth of stationery and three people have posted inappropriate content from office servers. It wouldn't help the company's reputation if that got out. Plus, you deal with large organisations and run their shopping sites and payment systems. The software you use is out of date.'

'But it cost us millions!'

'More fool you. It's for dinosaurs. It's at least three years old. You own an information technology firm that services thousands of retail businesses and designs new technology to streamline their administration. That needs constant updating. Don't you think that the payment systems need ongoing firewalling too?'

Connie was aghast. 'What does this all mean?'

'It means I'm keeping the house, but I won't charge you a fee for my services. Your system has made some accounts vulnerable.'

Connie almost choked on her wine. 'You can't be serious? That could ruin us. But whatever, that house is worth hundreds of thousands!'

Olivia shook her head in exasperation. 'So am I. I'm skilled and I charge a lot.' She paused. 'I used to... and now I am again. Anything over and above my fee I'll take because you tried to frame me, and my feelings are hurt.'

'Your feelings are hurt? You had a relationship with my husband!'

Olivia flushed. 'I slept with a single man I met in a bar. He was the liar, not me. You can't do what you did and get away with it.'

'*You* did.'

'I paid a price. I let you post videos of me online to make you feel better.'

Connie started sobbing and wiped her eyes on her sleeve. She reached for Darius but he shook her off, and led Olivia to the door. 'Let's go to the new house. We need to talk.'

Olivia just nodded and followed him to the car.

CHAPTER THIRTY-ONE

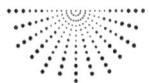

*O*livia sat unseeing as the world whizzed past the window. She'd usually tell Darius to slow down or to stop driving recklessly, but today she didn't care. She'd known the day would come when she'd have to confront Connie about her behaviour, but she hadn't expected it to be today. It was all too much.

Olivia had enjoyed having a friend of her own, for a short while, which was why she'd tried to bear what they were doing to her and pretend it wasn't happening. She'd been so sure that Connie would see the error of her ways once she knew the real Olivia, but perhaps that had been too much to hope for. The whole friendship was a sham and had been built on lies. What more could she expect? She'd lied about who she really was, too. Perhaps she deserved Connie's damnation.

Darius swung into the driveway of the big house and she felt a fat tear slide out of her eye and slosh onto her arm. She sniffed and wiped it away, groggily opening the door before Darius could do it for her and handing him the key to the front door. She didn't bother telling him the alarm code – he would already know it.

She followed him inside while he silenced the alarm and would have slumped to the floor if he hadn't swung her up into his arms, which was no mean feat. He carried her into the kitchen and gently placed her on the couch. The dogs weren't arriving back until the next day, so the space was eerily quiet. She supposed this was what it must have been like for Connie, when she came to the house to set her plan in motion. *How she must hate me.*

Darius settled her comfortably, then went to fill the kettle with water and waved his hand at the wall to turn the radio on. Olivia tried not to giggle at this and he hid a smile.

'How many times have you been inside this house?'

He paused for a fraction too long. 'Not many…'

He glanced at the little flashing red light and leaned in to pull a tiny wire out of the side of the camera.

'It's funny how you liked watching me at first, but now you don't want it to record our conversation?'

'I was checking up on you.'

'By hacking the feed?'

'I wanted to see what Connie was up to… once I realised who she was and what that meant.' He looked at his feet and kicked the board under one of the cupboards, but it was so well made it didn't budge.

'You wanted to spy on me and she gave you the perfect opportunity.'

He had the grace to look ashamed. 'Your dad had just died and you were avoiding everyone. Except Greg, who was married,' he said under his breath but she heard him well enough.

'I didn't know he was married! If you knew, *you* could have told me!'

'You wouldn't talk to me.'

'I was in pain, and Greg distracted me from my real life. I thought he was my hero – until he dumped me for someone else. I needed him, or I thought I did. At the time, he filled the void left by Dad.'

'I could have filled that void!' his voice rang out across the room and his fists were bunched. He started pacing around the kitchen and kicked the board again. Then he came and stood in front of her, eyes blazing, hair unkempt.

She pushed herself up and took his hands, drawing him onto the couch next to her. 'You are the only real family I have left. You're too precious to fall in love with and ruin our friendship. You're like a brother to me.'

He dropped her hand as if it had scalded him and turned away. 'I'm not your brother, though, am I?'

She faltered. They'd never actually said these words out loud and her heart felt like it was breaking into a thousand shards. 'Perhaps if I hadn't met Gabe, and if Connie didn't worship the ground you walk on, then things could have been different, but I don't think so.' She touched his arm to make him turn and face her. 'I love you more than anyone alive, Darius, just not the way you want me to.'

He pulled her into his arms and his lips founds hers. For a second she responded and kissed him back, but she braced her arms into his chest and then gently pushed him away. His eyes were pleading and she could feel his heart beating almost out of his chest, where her hands were resting. She saw tears form and he angrily brushed them away and sat back and stared at her.

'Gabe will break your heart.'

She drew in a shaky breath, never taking her eyes from his. 'He won't.'

'He's undercover Police. He's been watching you for ages. He thinks you're a drug dealer.'

She watched him wait for her to explode and to jump up

and shout and berate Gabe, but she stayed still, watching him. The victorious gleam in his eye faded and confusion took hold. Then he drew in a deep breath and slumped back into the folds of the couch, rubbing his temples. Finally he laughed out loud, almost wildly. 'Oh, Olivia... only you.'

'It's my job to know what's been going on. People pay me to be vigilant. I might be in mourning, but I'm not dead.' She leaned back too and tilted her head to look at his flushed, handsome face.

'He's been playing you.'

'Because you set him up to? You tipped him off when Connie wouldn't, and wanted to watch me get into trouble just as much as she did. Both of you have been having a fine time at my expense.' She sat up and shouted at him this time. 'I could have gone to jail, Darius!'

He hung his head and moved to the edge of the couch opposite her. 'You called the police and tipped them off that someone was growing drugs, didn't you?' she demanded to know. When he was silent, she had her answer. 'Connie didn't have the balls to do it, so you did it for her.'

'I saw she was setting you up and I actually thought that she deserved a little retribution. She was his wife and you were falling for him.'

'Darius! You are the last one to talk about people paying for what they have done. Connie's married!' She was almost baring her teeth at him now, and wished the dogs were there to rip his guts out, or lick him to death – which was more likely. 'She didn't follow through with her plan, so you did?' Olivia stood up and put her hands on her hips, glaring at him.

'I didn't know you'd like the guy they sent to watch you, did I?'

Olivia almost spat at him. 'That makes a difference? How

funny that you wanted to drag me from the throes of passion with one man and literally threw me into the waiting arms of another.' He flinched and his mouth set into an angry line. 'Was that why you did it? You're as bad as Connie.'

He looked up at her and she finally saw his reason. She'd always known it, but she'd done what she always did and covered for his bad behaviour. He tried to speak but she held her hand up to silence him. 'You did it so that you could rescue me, didn't you?' Bloody hell, Darius! Supposing they hadn't let me out?'

'I just wanted you to need me, for once,' he tried to capture her hand, but she shook him off and walked over to gaze unseeingly out of the wall-to-ceiling garden doors. Then she stalked back and swung her arm to punch him, but he caught her and pulled her onto his lap, his head pressed into her shoulder, until she gently pushed him away. All the fight had left her. She closed her eyes and started shaking.

'I'll always need you. You're my family.'

He pressed his forehead to hers, but said sadly, 'You don't need anyone. You wouldn't let me help pay for your dad's care. He was more of a dad to me than my own useless father. I wanted to help, but you shut me out. You weren't the only one who missed him or was grieving. I wanted you to notice me,' he spoke quietly and her bottom lip quivered, until sense and rage returned. She glared at him.

'By having me locked away!'

'I wouldn't have let it get to that. I would have hacked the documents or something, and changed them back to Connie's name.'

She threw her hands up in exasperation. 'No you wouldn't. You like her.'

He stood up, facing her. 'Ok, but I would have deleted the charge somehow.'

'See! You would have thrown me under the bus, but not Connie. Maybe you like her more than you think, you dumb-ass! You can't delete a police charge, however good you are at hacking. They would have noticed, or had other paperwork somewhere.'

'It all got out of hand. I don't like Connie that way,' he said, pleading with her.

'You absolute numb-nuts. You've been so busy plotting, you haven't realised that you actually like someone.'

'I was just playing with her to make you jealous. I wouldn't have let you go to jail.'

'It's me who won't let you go to jail,' she said quietly, the feeling of wanting to annihilate him leaving her suddenly. She pulled out a stool at the breakfast bar and he followed suit, staying hitting distance apart.

'What do you mean?'

'Who do you think has been keeping the police off your back for all these years? You've become sloppy. You think you're a master, but you're not. You think you're above the law – but you're not.'

He frowned and turned to face her as she went on. 'You think you are on a crusade to make the world a better place and to protect the women from the shelter, but you take for yourself too. You steal from these people, even though they might deserve it for hurting someone else. It's got to stop.'

When he tried to say something, Olivia held up her hand. 'You couldn't have believed it would go unnoticed, or that they wouldn't report it.'

'Those people were too arrogant to report it!'

'That's the problem with you, Darius. You aren't careful enough. You make mistakes. Some of your targets were so pompous that they assumed the police would just look at their own current predicaments and not check out their past.

But the police did both. They knew the women you were trying to protect had been embarrassed by having photos posted online first, then money went missing from the bank accounts of the people who had posted the photos. They realised it was some sort of payback.'

'Sometimes I just borrowed some money,' said Darius. 'I used it to fund a project to make money for the women's shelter, then when I got paid, I put it back. It was like a loan. It's why the targets didn't come forward... I thought. It was justice. Their money was paying for the women they hurt to rebuild their lives. I set up a fund for them. It's helped so many women.'

'A loan without the target's consent, or without them knowing it was going to be paid back? You used them, like they used other people.'

Darius stood up and paced over to the kitchen cupboards, opening and closing them with a bang, until he found two glasses and one of the bottles of wine Olivia had treated herself to the night before, when she'd decided she would move in. 'They needed to pay for what they did.'

'And it was up you to decide what they should pay?'

'No-one else was going to do it. It was about time they felt the same pain and humiliation their girlfriends or wives had felt when their photos were posted. I hit them where it would hurt them most – their wallets. And it stopped them doing it again to someone else.'

Olivia took the glass of wine he offered her and slugged some down, almost choking, as it was a lot stronger than the usual bottle she bought for a few pounds. 'That is one thing I do agree on. But you took it too far. And look at you now. You've tried to use me for your own purposes... All of you have. Even Gabe.'

Darius put his glass down and took hers from her. He

held her hands and looked at her, his eyes beseeching her. 'I love you.'

She shook his hands off while her cheeks flushed. 'You just love yourself.' She grabbed her wine back and took another hefty slug.

'What about Gabe? How come you aren't throwing things at him and telling him to get lost? He's used you from the moment you met him. He thinks you're a drug dealer!'

'He hasn't used me as much as I've used him.'

Understanding dawned and Darius snarled and threw the bottle into the sink, where it cracked and the wine poured away down the plug hole. 'What the hell…?'

'I've always known who he is,' confirmed Olivia. 'He's the contact I have at the police. I've been giving him tipoffs about company fraud to divert attention away from your bloody mistakes! It's given me time to cover your tracks as best I can. They know what you're doing, they just don't know who you are… yet.'

Darius paced over to the couch and sank into it, closing his eyes and rubbing his neck with his hand. 'Oh hell. I'm sorry, Libby. I thought I was so careful.'

'You were distracted. I understand. Dad's death hit you hard too, but you've become your own worst enemy. You're trying to make those awful people pay to cover your grief. Why can't you just get drunk and have sex in cars with inappropriate people, like the rest of us?'

His head shot up and he looked at her, before they both burst out laughing. She joined him on the couch and her head nestled on his shoulder.

'Seriously,' she told him. 'You have got to stop this now. You've got enough money to make your investments legitimately.'

'I like my job.'

'You like the buzz and attention. Turn that to a different cause.' He gently lifted her face up with his hand and gave her a wolfish grin, which melted her heart. Why couldn't she stay mad at this man? 'Not me! I am not your good cause.'

He sighed sadly. 'I like looking after you.'

'I've been looking after myself for longer than you, remember?' she huffed. 'And I've been looking after you, too.' He had the grace to sweep his sooty lashes across his eyes and not try to argue for a split second, then his eyes were open and the fire was back. 'Gabe lied to you.'

'So did you, so did Connie.'

'You slept with her husband.'

'Not intentionally! I've been trying to make it up to her ever since.' She looked around at the room that was now so familiar. She would definitely soften up the edges and make it more homely. 'I'm keeping the house, though.'

'What? Seriously?'

She grinned. 'Yep.'

'How can you do that? Surely that makes you as bad as me?'

'Nope. Connie put it in my name to get me arrested. She's got more money than sense.' When she saw his hackles rising slightly, she grinned at that too. 'I'm keeping the dogs, too, whatever she says.'

'What?' He turned to face her.

'She got them from a shelter by offering to walk them for a few hours a day, then left them here for me to make myself look stupid with. They've been running her ragged, but I love them.'

'What are you going to do about the videos?' He stared at her in awe. She had a secret smile on her face that only he understood. The one that came from making her tormentor pay. He'd seen it many times over the years, when people had tried to bully her at school. She'd always come out on top somehow. She was resourceful. He'd learnt a lot from her in those early days. She'd stuck up for him, too, when kids had poked fun at them for not having two parents at home, when the one he did have was useless, making him turn up to class with dirty clothes and ill-fitting shoes with holes in them. He'd tried to fight them but Olivia had made them pay a different way. She outsmarted them at every turn until they all wanted to be her friend.

When she didn't answer, he got up to retrieve the bottle from the sink, then wrinkled his nose at the mess and went to find a fresh one. 'Sorry about the wine. I'll buy you a new supply as a house-warming gift.' He topped up his glass, took a sip, and stared down at her. 'Why did you let her post stuff online, if you knew?'

Olivia giggled and peeked at him from over the rim of her glass. 'At first I felt I deserved it and it was my penance for being with Greg, however unintentionally. Then it went on for such a long time without her facing up to me about it, so I decided to enjoy it.'

Getting up and gesturing for Darius to follow, she took him all the way upstairs to the third floor, where for once it didn't feel like a furnace. Darius gasped when she swung open the door. Not just because of the racks and racks of empty wooden plant tables and heat lights that were strung across the centre of the huge room, which spanned the whole top of the house, but because of the furniture piled all around it.

He pulled her inside, and they both bumped into each other, laughing. 'You didn't?'

'I did.'

'They gave you all of this?'

'Yep, and more at the flat. Where do you think my new bed and all my flashy new clothes have been coming from?'

'These companies want you to make more dog videos, with their products in them?'

'Yes. Freebies!' They both roared with laughter. He kissed her hand and bowed down to her with a flourish.

'I just have to change the furniture and drop in how amazing it is, from time to time. My dog videos are pretty popular.'

His eyes narrowed for a second. 'Is that the real reason why you need the dogs?'

She stopped laughing and leaned against the wall, which she would soon be painting a refreshing shade of sky blue, and looked around at her hoard of designer furniture. She decided she might even hand-paint some tiny stars on the ceiling and lie there with the dogs, daydreaming.

'Nope.' She sighed and stood back up, pulling him with her. His arm slipped easily round her waist and she didn't slap him away. 'I really love those dogs. They need a home and so do I. I've just been existing for years. This is as good a place as any to rebuild my life. A new and better version.'

'You're really keeping the house?'

'I deserve it, after what she put me through. She can afford it.' Olivia didn't bother to go into detail about the deal she'd done with Greg to work for Connie's company as a consultant, to balance out some of the cost of the house. That was all she was prepared to give – nothing more. Greg had been so horrified by the whole sorry mess when she'd told him, the day before, that he'd almost offered her the house to buy her silence, but hadn't had the courage to completely follow through and face the wrath of his wife. And it was clear he hadn't had it out with Connie yet. He'd had to fly straight out on urgent business, as a meeting he'd forgotten about had suddenly appeared in his diary, after Olivia had taken a look at it, online. Weird, that…

She might tell Darius how much work she was prepared

to put in to help Connie's company survive another time but, for now, it was good to feel he was in awe of her for once. He pulled her to him and his hands captured her face. A tear slid from her eyes and he stepped away, brushing it aside with his thumb. Kissing her nose and taking her hand, he led her back downstairs and went to find that fresh bottle of wine.

CHAPTER THIRTY-TWO

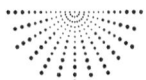

*G*abe had been trying to call Olivia for days now, and was starting to worry. She usually answered his texts or picked up his calls, but now there was just silence. Something was wrong. He didn't want to crowd her, but he missed talking to her. They had been speaking most days for a while. He hadn't pushed it, thinking she might need space. It went against all his instincts, though. He was getting restless. It was probably why he'd ended up working with his informant, Razor, instead of using the proper protocols. Using informants worked quickly and solved the problem effectively… except for the time he'd been shot. He'd taken unnecessary risks and had paid for them. He wouldn't be that careless again.

He had tried to brush the fact that there were procedures for a reason under the carpet, and forget about them. But more and more lately, he wondered if he had made the right choice. He was back working on the Damsel phishing hacker case, but over the last few weeks, the trail had cooled off. It was almost as if the person who had set the targets up was having a holiday from it all again. Gabe was pretty sure he'd be back, though. He'd been doing it for far too long to stop now, a bit like an addict who would always need a fix.

He pulled his phone from his jeans pocket and walked to close the office door and look out at the car park below. People were rushing about their business and were oblivious to the man in the window, watching them. He was back where he belonged. He'd just cracked a huge case and his boss had slapped him on the back and shaken his hand, offering his old office back.

Gabe had taken it, of course, but was still disgruntled that he'd been scolded like a child for using his initiative in his other work. Funnily enough it had been the tipoff from his source about the gang operating in the area that had changed things. He was pretty sure now that the criminal gang that Razor had told him about weren't involved in the Damsel bank thief scam, but they had been working towards an online fraud from several information technology companies locally who were growing so fast that they had forgotten to tighten up their own security. They all used a high tech programme that the gang members had worked out how to bypass. If they had gone through with the scam, then some of the country's biggest shopping sites would have had some serious questions to answer about their online safety standards. Their brands would have been damaged and the IT companies would have flatlined. Who the hell would have thought that people working in tech would overlook their own protocols? The criminal gang had, obviously. They probably even had people on the inside doing menial jobs. An image of Olivia and the stationery cupboard she'd described came to mind, but he brushed it aside.

He guessed that was why people paid a lot of money for the services of someone like her, to make sure that they were ahead of any technological developments. One part of an industry couldn't be assumed to be a master of all, it seemed.

He didn't care as it had done him a favour. It had led him to be able to offer a tipoff to their own computer geniuses, without having to ask them to do something outside of their job description, and had got him his office back. He'd like to buy his informant a drink and say thanks, as he hadn't asked for anything in return… yet, but Gabe was sure he'd surface when he wanted the debt to be repaid.

Enjoying the fact that his leg was finally healing and didn't hurt him every time he moved, he grinned and decided regular love-making had been the perfect rehabilitation. Not only had his colleagues mentioned that he must be getting some, as his mood had lifted and he even smiled at people occasionally and asked after their families, but he was working more efficiently and was back on form.

Checking his phone again and feeling a slight pang that there weren't any text messages from Olivia, he thought for a moment and then typed a message. He also quickly sent a mail to ask if his source had any news of the Damsel hacker, but it immediately bounced back. Before he had time to think, his phone pinged and he was called into a meeting. He quickly sent another text to Olivia asking how she was, and was gratified finally to get a response, asking him to meet her. He took one more glance and then his step faltered, as he saw the address she had sent him. It was the big house, with a time of seven that evening.

~

*I*t felt weird to drive up to the front of the house in a taxi and not park along the street and spy on people coming and going, not that he'd ever spotted anyone other than Olivia. When he pressed the intercom, she opened the door almost immediately and the two dogs from the video barked and danced around their feet. She grabbed onto their collars and laughed, shushing them. What the hell was going on?

She was glowing, with dewy skin and sparkling eyes. Her wide black trousers swished around her legs and she was wearing a silky top with little flowers sprinkled all over, tied in a knot at her midriff. Her hair was freshly cut and she even had subtle but oh-so-sexy make-up on. Her lips were shiny and inviting. He leaned in to kiss her, but she was pulled by one of the dogs and he missed and got her cheek.

She hoisted the dogs back towards what he assumed was the kitchen and he followed in awe, taking in the rich colours of the fabrics lining the windows and the cushions on the chairs. There was an oversized, shocking pink couch along the far wall. He frowned. It wasn't the one from any of the dancing dog videos he'd watched, over and over again, trying to see if anything in the house held a clue to the original cannabis complaint. There had been nothing, but in the end he'd watched the clips again and again because they were funny – and in a couple of them she'd been in her bra, which was always a good thing.

He stopped for a moment as the thought struck him that millions of other people had also seen her in her bra, but he shook it off. Her face hadn't been showing, and only he was allowed close enough to actually touch her... he hoped. He wondered if she finally trusted him enough to tell him about her Internet business, and her old job come to that. He wanted her to trust him and tell him the truth about her life. Then he winced, as she still didn't know the real him.

He looked out onto a manicured lawn and one of the dogs ran over and started jumping up at his legs. She called it away, but it was actually quite cute for a huge dog and Gabe scratched behind its ears until the dog calmed down.

'He likes you,' Olivia smiled.

Gabe couldn't help but grin back. She was looking sensational and all he really wanted to do was ravish her on the kitchen floor. 'I like dogs. What is this place?' he gestured to the garden and huge hallway they had just walked through. 'Is it where you work?'

She laughed gaily and handed him a glass of wine. His eyes narrowed and his gut tightened. She was behaving decidedly oddly. Had she met someone else, and just asked him here to tell him face to face? Perhaps it was the guy who had bought the house for her, if she had moved back in. It looked like she had, from the photos of her dad and Darius that were carefully placed around the room in beautiful frames. He didn't see any of another man, though.

A flicker of hope sprung up and he walked towards her and took her free hand. She sipped her wine and studied him, then seemed to make a decision and put both their glasses down, and led him upstairs.

As they climbed higher and higher to the top of the house, he started to hope that she was going to have her wicked way with him, but those hopes were dashed when he saw what was inside the door she swung open. Racks and racks of heaters and plant trays. His mind went blank for a second and he stared around him like a moron, as he'd really believed the tipoff was fake. What a crap detective he was, and what the hell did this mean for them? Was she a drug dealer after all? Had he been so wrong about her? Finally his eyes narrowed and his forehead creased. He walked further into the room and inspected the racks. They looked fairly new and none of the lamps were on. There were no plants here, just what looked like a huge pile of furniture, packing and torn labels. He turned to face her, a million questions on his tongue.

'What is this?'

'Don't you know?'

His stomach plummeted. 'Uh… it looks like racks for growing cannabis to me. Why are they in this house?'

She walked over and trailed her fingers along part of the wood, letting her hand drop and rest by her side. Her eyes were troubled too and she brushed her hair out of her face and stood in front of him. 'Well, they're here for growing cannabis.'

'What? What the hell are you talking about?' He walked around, picking up discarded plant pots and throwing them back down again. 'Who is growing cannabis? You? Your employer? Whose house is this?'

'You know it's my house, and I know you think I'm a drug dealer,' she said quietly, standing and staring out of the window in the eaves, which looked out onto fields and beautiful woodland beyond. 'Or some sort of computer hacker who steals money from people. You haven't quite worked that bit out yet.'

Gabe was floored. This was his worst nightmare. He tried to take her hand and make her look at him, but she stayed staring into the distance, a statue of ice that he couldn't reach. 'Look… Libby…' She gave him a sharp look and he drew a breath and held it.

He closed his eyes for a second and tried to think about how the hell she knew who he was. Had she always known…? Then it hit him square between the eyes. Yes. She had always known. The pain in his leg returned and he flinched. 'You dated me to see how much I knew about the hacker?'

She didn't give anything away. '*You* dated me to find the hacker in the first place… and the bloody weed factory.'

'I didn't,' he protested, kicking the bottom of a wooden rack and making it wobble.

He stomped down the stairs, feeling really used, and went to grab his coat from the kitchen. The dogs immediately bounded over and demanded strokes and tickles. He tried to push them away, but they were huge. She called them and they immediately sat down. 'When the hell did they become so bloody well behaved?'

She waltzed past him and stuck her nose in the air, her skin flushed. 'So you've seen the dog videos too?'

He slammed his coat back down on the kitchen surface. 'Of course I have. You're an Internet sensation. Everyone's seen them. I was waiting for you to tell me about them, and this house, and the flat!'

'The same way I've been waiting for *you* to tell me you really work for the Police and have been watching me for months because someone paid you to.'

His face blanched and then screwed up in anger. She was infuriating. 'I didn't know I was going to fall in love with you, did I?' he shouted, making her, the dogs, and a lone pigeon who had just walked up outside the window, stop and freeze.

She flushed and her eyes blazed with anger too. 'Is that another standard line you use to win over your undercover targets?'

'Of course not! I mean it. I wasn't undercover. I was just curious... and I liked you. I'd been shot because I hadn't followed procedures at work and was put on desk duty. I was bored and lonely until I met you.'

She brushed past him and he caught her arm and stopped her. 'So you weren't casing my flat or digging for information about my past, in case I happened to be some uber-coder who borrows money from rich people who post hate photos online?'

'It started that way, but that's not what it is now.' He wanted to be honest, but also to keep her in his life. He was at a loss as to what to do, so he pulled her body to his and kissed her. She returned his passion with a fire of her own and filled his body with longing. His hands ran along her waist and around her backside and she growled and then broke away from him, her lips plump and glistening.

'This whole 'relationship' has been built on lies.' She said the word *relationship* as if it disgusted her.

He captured her hands and kissed them gently. 'I'm sorry if I lied. I was given a tipoff about this house and its owner. I came and watched a few times for paperwork's sake. I didn't see anything suspicious, but I did see you. That was my downfall. I couldn't stop coming back after that. I'd shut the case, and then information I'd requested came in about you and your dad. And your old job and this house. It didn't add up.'

She was shaking and he put his arms around her and led her to the couch. He sat beside her and the dogs immediately came over and slumped at their feet. He could imagine what it would be like to have a family like this, and it made him feel like an idiot for not telling her the truth. The problem was he'd got in so deep, it was hard to dig himself out.

'You used my dad as a way in. Your nan, too,' she said sadly. 'I liked you.'

He took in a gulp of air. 'You lied to me, too. You said you were a dog sitter and worked in a stationery cupboard.'

'That was the truth.'

'You own this house, though. Why live in the flat? What are the racks for upstairs?' he felt his heart rate ramp up. If she was a criminal, they were in trouble. 'Plus my nan is real.'

'I know. I looked her up.'

Gabe paused for a moment and then burst out laughing, and she looked at him under her lashes and smiled. Man, he wanted to kiss her again, but he daren't push his luck too far in case she threw him out, or fed him to the dogs.

'Connie did all of this. Darius, too. They wanted to get me into trouble,' Olivia said sadly.

'What? You can't be serious. Why? They're your best friends. Darius is your family!'

He jumped to his feet and the dogs sprang up, barking. She grabbed them and shushed them with a gentle tone and then got up herself to flick the kettle on, then seemingly decided to grab a beer for him and a glass of wine for herself instead. That meant he would be staying for at least another fifteen minutes, so he tried to calm down. She handed him the beer and he gulped it down his parched throat. This wasn't the way he'd envisaged his day. He'd hoped they wouldn't have got much farther than the bed.

'What has Connie got to do with cannabis? I can't imagine her lighting up a spliff.' He laughed, and then stopped at the sight of her serious face.

CHAPTER THIRTY-THREE

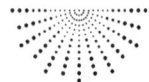

*O*livia tucked her legs up on her brand new couch and tried not to sink into its welcoming comfort too much. She was exhausted from talking to Gabe, but was determined not to let him off the hook, or let him kiss her any more. She completely lost her senses when he did that and she needed to stay sharp. She was so mad at him and had been since the start, but she'd hoped and prayed that one day he would tell her the truth. That day had never arrived and she was tired of waiting.

The wall of ice around her heart had melted a bit when he'd said he loved her, but how could she trust a word that came out of his mouth?

Ok, she'd lied too, but that was more withholding information than bare-faced fabrications. He'd told her he worked as a consultant. She seethed. Darius was probably right, and he was just after one thing. To be honest, that was all she'd been after at the start. She'd wanted to show people that she was good enough for a gorgeous man like Gabe to want to date.

She looked at him. He was still waiting for her answer.

She hated how pliable she was when he was near. She was using all her willpower not to stroke his face or pull herself into his warm lap and curl into his body. She knew he still fancied her by the way he kissed her, but was that enough? Could they stop lying to each other? Darius was the big setback to that plan, and always would be. One man in her life was a master criminal, or used to be, and one worked for the Police.

She rolled her neck and tried to get more comfortable. She'd worn clothes to intimidate him but it seemed that they just turned him on. To be fair, anything she did seemed to turn him on. She couldn't help a secret smile and he cocked his head in question.

'I had a very brief relationship Connie's husband.' He certainly hadn't expected that and hadn't done his home-work, by the look of shock on his face. She held up a hand to stop his questions. 'He lied to me. We dated for a while and I didn't find out he was married until it was too late.'

'But she's your friend,' he sounded horrified, which put her back up immediately and she got up to grab her wine. She plonked herself on a kitchen stool and swung to face him.

'Don't judge me. I wasn't her friend then and I thought Greg and I were both single.'

'Then how…?'

'She found out about Greg and I and decided that I must be the love of his life, for some reason.' When he tried to speak again, she cut him off. 'It made her double guess herself, and she decided to befriend me when she discov-ered I was working with him. He'd spun both of us, so many lies.' She sipped her wine, but even the heavenly fragrance and rich grapes couldn't lift her spirits. 'I didn't apply for the job knowing he was there. It was just a cruel coinci-dence. He was as repelled as I was. It was so embarrassing.

197

He'd dumped me when I was at my lowest and it hurt like hell.'

Gabe didn't look happy, but went and helped himself to another beer and came and sat next to her, taking a long cooling sip and waiting to hear more.

'She had a deranged plan to try and get me into trouble for growing cannabis in my own home, so she bought a load of plants off of some guy on the Internet, put the house in my name, hired me to do the dog sitting job, and was going to report me.'

'Some bloke off the Internet delivered cannabis plants?' He was incredulous.

Olivia rolled her eyes. 'I know! They were plants that looked similar and most were half dead, when I finally got in there. She hadn't bothered to check if they were real, or ask herself why someone would sell them to her. Like I said, she's deranged, but to be fair I'm not sure what I'd do in her position. She was hurting pretty badly and not thinking straight. She assumed that punishing 'the other woman', would ease her own pain,' she sighed. 'It didn't.'

'Was she the one who did report it?'

'No, she chickened out. That was Darius,' she said sadly. That still hurt like hell and Darius was now ignoring her, even though she was the wronged one. He'd apologised when he'd finally left. She'd thought they'd ironed most things out and left on good terms, but she'd been wrong. She hadn't heard from him at all. She knew he was bruised too, but he'd cut her out of his life.

'Darius? Why the hell would he do that? He loves you more than life itself.'

Her skin flushed a deep red and she hid her face behind her wine glass. 'Is it that obvious?'

'Of course!' he raged, swinging his beer bottle around and making her cringe in case it ruined her beautiful kitchen. He hadn't bothered with the glass this time. 'What were they playing at?'

'She wanted to get me in the maximum amount of trouble, to pay me back for my relationship with Greg.'

'But a house? Who buys a house to get someone into trouble?'

'Someone with more ready cash than sense. Her whole family have been pandering to her for years. She could afford a hundred houses like this. She thinks she's come up with all the money-making ideas for her parents' company, but in fact Greg has been protecting her for years. Her designs are terrible! She's got no idea what she's doing, whereas he… he's actually a very talented programmer in his field and he's the reason the company's value has grown steadily. She's so self-obsessed that she doesn't even notice him, unless he's doing something wrong. So he started doing that, more and more. It's a complete mess. He still loves her, but then Darius got involved and now she's obsessed with him instead.'

'Darius and Connie?'

'Yep.' She made a sick face and he laughed. She liked the sound of his laughter and felt some of the earlier tension easing from her bones. She enjoyed talking to Gabe, even when she hated him.

'The videos?'

'She put up a sign asking for a dog sitter where she knew I'd see it. She had a friend who worked at a dog shelter and these two were high maintenance and really naughty, so she offered to take them out for a few hours during the week,' said Olivia. 'But the dogs are gorgeous and just wanted company. The only thing they destroyed were the stupid outfits she left out for them. They hated them and chewed them to bits.'

His mouth fell open and she giggled and threw the wine cap at him. 'She knew I needed money, as I was working as a very efficient and important pen supervisor,' she gave him a warning look when he was going to laugh about this. He'd always teased her about that job, but she'd quite enjoyed it in the end. 'She wanted to humiliate me. She wrote out games for me to play with the dogs so I'd have to make an idiot of myself. She set up the video feed, but didn't check it once she'd met me.'

'She liked you.' He stated the fact, as if everything was unravelling in his mind now. 'She didn't report you, either, because you became true friends.'

'She got me to spy on her husband, Greg, to make me realise I wasn't special and that he had other affairs, and took me to a hairdressers where she paid them extra to charge me a fortune and make me bald... down there!' she signalled with her eyes to her crotch and they both burst out laughing. She liked the deep timbre of his voice.

'Perhaps she felt she'd got her vengeance after that. But why would Darius get involved? Did he know she was setting you up?'

'He did, but he had his own agenda. I was lost without my dad and I turned to Greg for support and companionship, not him. He wanted to scare me away from that family.'

'You have got to be kidding! By getting you arrested?'

'Neither of them imagined it would come to anything. They thought I'd get slapped wrists and be embarrassed enough to leave quietly.'

'How can you ever speak to them again?' he frowned and sipped his beer, aimlessly rubbing Bertie's head as he sat by his feet, which she found quite amusing.

'I'm not sure about Connie, although I can see she was in a lot of pain. With Darius, he's my family. I know why he does what he does. He has to save women, but with me I was capable of saving myself, so he sabotaged my job instead. He wanted to get me away from Greg and Connie, at first.' She gazed out of the window at the slight breeze that was making her new plants sway in the wind. They looked like they were dancing. 'Everyone leaves Darius, except me, so he thinks that by expressing his love for me, he can keep me close. He doesn't realise that I'll never leave him.'

Gabe got up and gave her a hug, linking his arms around her waist and resting his cheek on her head. 'I'm sorry I lied to you, too. I didn't mean to, but I thought you'd run away if you realised I was looking into your life.'

She leaned back and looked at him. 'You thought I might be the Damsel phishing hacker you're looking for. You were worried I was stealing money to fund my lifestyle, then feeling guilty and putting it back.'

'How do you...?' The last detail wasn't public knowledge, and they hadn't discussed it when he'd joked about the article in the paper months before.

She held up her hands. 'It's not me.'

'Then how do you know the details of that case?' he picked up his phone and quickly typed a mail and sent it. A noise immediately pinged on Olivia's phone, which was sitting innocently on the counter. 'You're my source? You're the one who helped solve my cases? Razor?' He looked down at his leg and rubbed it. 'I took advice from another source and got shot. My bosses weren't happy with me working with a coder again, but had to admit it got results on the information technology companies case. Why do you do it?'

When she didn't answer, he realised the truth at last. 'You were protecting him, weren't you? You could have got into a lot of trouble. You still can, for interfering in things. And he'll get caught!'

This was the Gabe she had been waiting to see. The policeman, who would always put his job before her. She got up and called the dogs, walking to the door. 'I think you should leave.'

He didn't need asking twice, grabbing his coat and angrily storming out of the house. He stopped short when he saw a taxi waiting outside, the engine idling. She must have ordered it when they were on the third floor, knowing what she was going to tell him and how he'd react. Was he so predictable? His face flushed and he ground his teeth. He slammed the car door when he got inside, but that was lost on her as, after checking he was really leaving, she'd already stalked back inside to find her bottle of wine.

CHAPTER THIRTY-FOUR

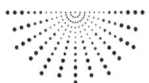

*D*arius was slobbing out across his couch, hair unkempt and food strewn all around him, when Olivia arrived. His personal assistant, Poppy, had let her in and rolled her eyes in his direction before leaving them to it. Olivia tiptoed her way across the usually pristine room and wrinkled her nose. She picked up a coffee cup and then drew back at the acrid smell. 'Darius. What's going on?'

He raised bloodshot eyes to her and then slumped back down.

'What is it?' she asked again, gingerly moving an old towel from the end of the couch and sitting down by his legs. 'I've never seen you like this before.' She nudged his feet to get his attention.

'Connie's gone back to Gorgeous Greg.'

'Connie? I thought you said you weren't interested in Connie?'

When he didn't answer, she nudged him again, but a lot harder this time, so he fell onto the floor with a bang. Poppy stuck her head round the door, and Olivia smiled and told her it was fine.

'He's been like this for weeks,' Poppy said helpfully. 'He's sacked most of his staff and the rest have walked out because he's so annoying,' she added, looking pointedly at Darius. He had the grace to look ashamed. Olivia thanked her and she went back to her work.

'You sacked your staff? Hire them back. They're like family. You trust them.'

'They hate me,' he said morosely. 'So do you, so does Connie. She said I love you so I can't like her.'

'Of course you love me. We're family. So you are properly interested in her now?'

'Only if she likes me,' he sulked. She gave him a dig in the ribs and he yelped.

'What's happened to make you so keen all of a sudden, when five minutes ago…'

He gave her a filthy look and she flushed. They hadn't seen each other since that day, or spoken. In the end, she'd had enough of his games and gone to see his mum. She'd told Olivia he'd been helping out more at the shelter and Connie had been there too. Maybe they were both paying their penance.

Joan had said she'd mentioned Olivia, but neither of them had wanted to talk about the situation. They spent hours discussing things in Winston's café instead, apparently. Joan didn't know what they were talking about, but they'd obviously grown close over their mutual evilness.

'So she's not interested in you romantically?' Olivia persisted. When Darius didn't look up, she sat down on the floor with him. 'How do you know?'

When he didn't answer, she slapped her palm against her forehead. 'Darius! You didn't hack her?'

He shrugged and she smacked his leg so he yelped and sat up groggily, clutching his forehead and closing one eye and then the other, before opening both. She spied an empty vodka bottle under the edge of the couch and heaved him up onto the seat.

'You can't hack into people's personal files, especially if you fancy them. How many times have I told you not to do this? No wonder you never stay with a woman, she can't have any secrets from you.'

'You have secrets from me,' he whined, looking around for the coffee cup that was normally by his side every minute of the day when he was working from home. Poppy walked in and placed a steaming fresh cup beside them both and gave Olivia a sympathetic and slightly hopeful smile. Olivia didn't know why everyone thought she could solve all Darius's problems. He was an idiot.

'To be clear… you've finally realised that you're not in love with anyone else and you like Connie?'

He sniffed his coffee appreciatively and took a tentative sip, before finally turning and looking at her. His ink-blue jeans had a small tear in one leg and his T-shirt was crumpled and splotched with stains. She didn't think she'd seen him like this since he'd lived with his dad. Olivia's dad had taken over cleaning and pressing his clothes not long after, as he'd been bullied for how messy he'd looked. Darius's dad hadn't minded someone else doing the work, as it had made him look as if he was doing a great job of looking after his son without any of the effort. He slept for most of the day, so he barely noticed what his son wore. He'd soon have noticed if social services had come knocking, though, but however much her dad had wanted to report him, Darius had begged him not to. He might have been taken far away from them and none of them could have borne that. Plus, Darius was always saying that his mum would be back soon. But she never did come back to the house.

Olivia brushed Darius's thick dark fringe away from his face and sighed. She had never been able to stay mad at him.

And she was a little bit relieved that they didn't have to talk about his feelings for her again.

He caught her hand and kissed it, the way he always had as they were growing up. A brotherly kiss. Then he placed her palm on his cheek. 'I'm sorry for putting you through all that. When your dad died all I could think of was losing you. I thought the way to keep you was to tell you I was in love with you. Well, I still love you,' he said sadly. 'But I know you're not in love with me. Spending time with Connie has made me realise that I can care about someone else. The way that I feel about her is weird, it's different. She makes me feel nervous, whereas when with you, I'm comfortable, like an old pair of socks.'

'Thanks… I think,' she bantered gently.

He sipped his coffee and stared out of the window. 'I'm starting to understand that there are other ways of loving people. I will always need you in my life, but I want her in it too. I know you hate us both, but she's misguided. Greg's done a complete number on her.'

When Olivia raised an eyebrow he grinned suddenly, and she couldn't help but grin back. My, she loved this man. 'Ok, they *are* both mad, but I kind of like her. Her ideas are atrocious, especially for work, and she needs to get control of her jealous behaviour…'

'Oh for goodness sake, Darius! She's a nightmare.' Olivia jumped up and stomped around the room, making Poppy stick her head round the door again and then leave them to it. 'Greg is a total pig, but she's overbearing, demanding and controlling. They deserve each other.' When his smile faded she bit her lip and stopped pacing. 'But you like her?'

He sighed and got up to face her. 'I do like her. More than I realised. You were right when you said we were suited. I need someone who is a bit feisty like you… and she needs someone who's not a doormat.'

'Ugh. It's disgusting. The thought of you together turns my stomach,' she teased him, only half-joking, 'but if that's what you both want, then go for it. Just stay out of my way, at least until I calm down and forget that you both tried to have me arrested.' She shot him a dagger glare, which he thoroughly deserved, and he looked wounded. 'How do you know she's back with Greg?'

'She told me she'd filed for divorce, but she's cancelled it.'

'You checked? Darius!'

He had the grace to look ashamed, but it wasn't convincing. 'Perhaps she's waiting for you to actually tell her how you feel? Have you said you like her?'

'Not really.'

'Oh, for goodness sake. No wonder she's giving him a second chance. She likes big gestures. He's probably bought her a castle.'

'I can buy her a castle,' he sulked.

'So go and buy her one, you idiot. Actually, don't. It's about time she learnt that money doesn't equate to love. Do something wildly romantic that Greg couldn't buy, with all the money in England.'

He looked like his brain was whirring, but then he smiled suddenly and she saw a glimpse of the gorgeous man she'd grown up with. 'I could do that, couldn't I?'

She smiled and kissed his cheek gently. 'Yes, you can. If it means that much to you and you really want a psychopath as a girlfriend.' He was about to rush away and begin planning, but she caught his hand. 'Gabe knows about you. In fact, he knows about me, too.'

He froze and his smile dropped. 'What is he going to do?'

'Honestly, I don't now. I've helped you as much as I can and I'm not sure what he could prove, but I'm positive there is someone smarter than me who can unravel everything I've done.'

'There's no one smarter than you with computers, Libby.'

She sighed. 'I wish that were true. I know I'm good, but there are loads who are probably better. I just have a head start as I've done this from such a young age and kept myself up to date. You've got to stop what you're doing now,' she pleaded. 'Think of another way to help the women at the shelter and to make money. You've got enough to last two lifetimes.' When he was about to speak, she held her hand up to stop him. 'Having the biggest bank balance around isn't going to make your mum notice you.' When his mouth fell open she carried on, knowing this was going to hurt. 'Perhaps she's not the person you want her to be, but she's the only mum you've got. At least she's around and she does care about you… in her own funny way.'

'Don't say that, she does care!' Darius protested.

'I know she does, but she should pay you more attention and that's her fault and not yours. Everyone loves you, Darius, you're adorable, when you're not causing havoc or being a pain in the arse. She thinks those women need her but she misses seeing how much you're hurt. I get so angry at her!'

He walked forward and pulled her into his arms, resting his head on the top of her hair. 'I didn't know you felt that way. I thought you liked her.'

'I love her, but I'm cross with her, too. I lived with your pain as if it was my own. It was as if both of our mums had died, but she was alive and could have helped us all. She chose to help herself.'

'My dad was a drunk and a wife beater.'

'I know that. I applauded her for having the strength to leave! It must have been the hardest day of her life. I was a child and was mad at her for leaving you behind, even though I tried to understand why. It was when she came back to face your dad when she was stronger, and still didn't take you with her, that I found it hard to forgive. She left you there, when she had a safe home, because she was busy with her new life. I know how much she means to you, but you suffered because of her too. I want her to find time for you now and not make it so that you have to go and make stupid jam in order to spend time with her.'

'I don't have to make jam, I like it.'

Olivia leaned her head back and looked up at Darius, and he flushed. 'Ok. I hate making jam. I am good at it, though.'

'Only because you've made about ten thousand jars,' she joked, poking him in the ribs and moving away. 'You've got to have a career change, for all our sakes. Please, Darius?'

He ran his hands through his hair, which she noticed needed cutting, and gave a slight nod of his head, before turning and walking purposefully towards his study.

CHAPTER THIRTY-FIVE

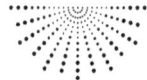

*D*arius had been turning up every few days to help
Olivia decorate the new house. He seemed
happier and she loved seeing him relaxed, even though he'd
gone back to pristine designer clothes and immaculate
swept-back hair. She'd tried to persuade him to wear overalls
over his jeans, but he'd refused and in Darius style had
managed to stay paint splotch-free. She wondered if that was
actually because he left her to do most of the work while he
lay on the floor playing with the dogs, or if he actually did all
the painting he said he did. He'd hired her a team of helpers,
as the house was huge, but she'd got rid of them after a few
days. She was gradually visiting shops and galleries and
finding her own style.

Her dog videos were still trending most weeks and she'd
been offered more sponsorship. The dogs now had scented
shampoos every few days and had several sparkly collars and
some pretty weird dog clothes. They seemed to love them all,
as these costumes actually fit them properly and were made
for dogs. She hoped they didn't become divas. The viewing
numbers were still growing. She was working closely with

several big firms to tighten up their security and had even been on a couple of dates. Her heart hadn't been in it, though, and she'd given up after the third man. He'd had bad breath and kept putting his hand on her leg, until she'd 'accidentally' kicked him in the shin.

She walked to the kitchen counter and flicked the switch to turn on her fancy new coffee machine, bending down to pet Bertie and Belle who had followed her and who had managed to get paint all over one side of their fur. 'Darius! You're supposed to be keeping the dogs away from the paint, you twit,' she laughed, grabbing a cloth and trying to wipe the sky blue colour away. It wasn't budging. Darius walked over and smothered a giggle. 'This is your fault,' she accused.

The doorbell rang and she looked at him pointedly until he shrugged and went to look at the intercom for the front door. She glanced under the cupboard where the tiny camera used to sit, and then behind her to the brand new filming setup that she had for her video channel. She'd had no idea how much work was involved in keeping an online presence that you actually wanted the world to see, but she was kind of enjoying it. She didn't feel isolated, even though she worked alone, or with a couple of furry and bouncy dogs. It paid well and gave her the freedom to choose her hours. She thought back to her days at her desk in the stationery cupboard and how much fun it had been to hack the system from an antiquated computer. If only they'd known what she'd found out about them all. Luckily she wasn't like Darius, or she'd have hung them out to dry for their lack of care and attention to their customers and, in their opinion, over-the-hill co-workers. They'd grown so fast that they'd become sloppy.

Still, she had a new home and career to keep her busy. She didn't need friends like the people who worked at Greg's firm. If they knew she was the dancing dog queen, they'd literally be all over her, of that she was sure, whatever her age or hairstyle. She thought back to the way Connie had made her get waxed and actually smiled. That girl had balls.

Hearing someone clear their throat behind her, she turned and almost fainted at the sight of Gabe in her kitchen. He looked tanned and gorgeous, like he'd been sitting on a beach for weeks, while she looked like she'd stuck her head in a pot of paint. Marvellous.

Darius hovered around, but she signalled it was ok and he lifted his phone up to show he was going to call Connie.

After his huge gesture of setting up a picnic and taking Connie boating on a lake had worked, and they'd decided to date each other, he'd been happy. He hadn't actually stuck to the rules of a cheap date, as he'd bought the picnic from an exclusive department store, had the lunch in a mooring on a private estate and then taken her aboard a yacht. But he had spent the day telling her how much she meant to him. She'd finally believed him and he'd actually dared to bring her to Olivia's home. She'd grovelled and said Olivia could keep the house, which was gracious as it was hers anyway.

Seeing Darius so content had softened Olivia's heart. She'd wondered if she'd feel jealous, but she'd just felt exhausted. She'd listened to them talk about their date and smiled in all of the right places, but it would take time for her to forget what both of them had done to her.

CHAPTER THIRTY-SIX

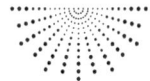

*G*abe almost sighed when he saw Olivia. He'd tried hard not to want to punch Darius when he'd opened the door. Darius was the reason for this whole mess. It had taken Gabe accepting a job abroad for a couple of weeks, to help a mate in trouble, to calm himself down. He'd called Olivia a hundred times, but in the end he'd always cut off before she answered. He couldn't understand why she'd protected a criminal, but it also left the question if she'd ever done anything illegal herself – and he was afraid to find the answers to that question. He knew she investigated companies, but that was all within the law as far as he could see. He was pretty sure she had underground contacts, but whether she used them or not couldn't be proved from the investigations he'd done.

The leads that had brought him nearer to Darius had all been dead ends and he'd stopped what he was doing for now. Perhaps Olivia had told Darius about Gabe being onto him, but then surely Darius wouldn't still be hanging around if she had. No one could be that cocky. Gabe had a sinking suspicion that was exactly what he was doing, *hanging around,* but he was also the best friend of the woman he loved, and her only family other than a random uncle, so he had to tread very carefully.

She looked adorable with paint-spiked hair and soft curves under a fitted T-shirt and rolled up jeans, giving him a glimpse of calf and prettily painted pink toenails. He gulped in some air, as she was standing and staring at him without saying anything. The dogs came in from the garden and raced over to see him, jumping up and almost knocking him over. He laughed and bent down to ruffle their fur, breaking the tension. 'I wasn't sure you'd let me in.'

'I didn't, Darius did.' He looked up at her from his place beside the dogs and she rolled her eyes and went to grab a bottle of wine and some beers. He noticed they were his favourite brand and got up to accept one, his hand brushing hers, the electricity making them both jump. He looked around for Darius and, when he saw he was still on the phone at the end of the garden, he took Olivia's hand and led her to the couch. He admired the way she'd changed the house. It was full of life and colour now, and even the front had been softened by bursts of foliage and flowers.

'You look like you've been on holiday.' She tried to hide the accusation in her voice but he heard it.

'A friend abroad asked for my help and I needed an excuse to drop the case I was working on and to hand it to someone else.'

She went white and put her wine down on the little silver side table.

'It's ok,' he added. 'It wasn't going anywhere. The criminal who was doing it was clever and completely deleted all traces of it ever happening. Monies have been paid back and, for a reason that I'm sure someone knows, but I don't want to know, the people who made the complaints all went away. Each case was dropped. I have no idea how it was done, but it was. They all withdrew their cases while I was away. It's as if the whole thing never happened.'

He looked at her closely, but she was at just as much of a loss as he was. They both looked into the garden and Darius smiled and waved while he chatted away. They both gawped and then looked at each other, before bursting out laughing. 'Someone's back on form,' she joked.

When Gabe tried to move closer, she gave him a warning stare. 'I'm still mad at you. I haven't heard from you for ages.'

Gabe wished he'd had the courage not to cut the calls, all those times he'd rung her. 'I heard you've been busy dating…'

She flushed and grabbed her wine, but he took it from her and placed it beside her on the table.

'You've been spying on me again?'

He slipped his arm around her and pulled her onto his lap as she squealed in surprise. He stroked a stray hair out of her eyes, but it was stuck with paint and sprang back, almost poking his eye out as he brushed her lips with his. She didn't shy away, but bit his lip and made him groan. He looked into the garden again and she followed his eyeline. 'Darius told you?'

'He said all your dates were boring and vulgar and I was the best out of a bad bunch. He also said that if I was going to wait much longer you'd be snapped up by one of the millionaire clients who shower you with gifts and that I should get over myself and stop sulking.'

'Oh,' she giggled into his neck, her warm breath making him scoop her further into him. He noticed that Darius was walking around the building towards the side gate and hoped he was going home.

'He also met and spoke to me off the record about his work. He told me not to worry,' he said, exasperated. 'He said you'd made him see the light and Connie had threatened to chop his nether regions off if he ever broke the law again, so he'd put things right and it was about time I did the same, if I was man enough.'

Olivia burst out laughing and the dogs piled on top of them and tried to lick their faces. Gabe stood up with her in his arms and the dogs fell away. He kissed her lips, then her neck and her face and then placed her bottom on the kitchen counter while he ravaged her mouth, his hands tracing the contours of her hips and backside. She ignited in his arms and they both lost themselves in each other before coming up for air, arms still entwined.

He looked into her eyes and smiled. 'I'm sorry for lying to you. I was annoyed at being demoted, and then saw you going into this house. There was nothing to go on, but you already had me from that moment. I used work as an excuse to see you, but then had to hide who I was. The more important you became to me, the bigger the lie grew and the more desperate I was to keep it going. I couldn't face losing you, but it happened in the end anyway.'

She slipped her hands round to the back of his waist and they dipped into his jeans, making him gasp in some air and pull her hips to his.

'You didn't lose me. I've always been yours.'

He reached for her and lifted her into the air, while she wrapped her legs around him. He strode up the stairs and swung her bedroom door shut behind them. Then he walked them into the shower and turned it on full blast. As it soaked through their clothes, he peeled the layers from their skin until they were chest to chest and heart to heart.

Touching her face, he looked into her eyes and smiled, as he ran his other hand along her soft skin, making her sigh with pleasure. Kissing his way around her face and body, he told her over and over again how much she meant to him and they lost themselves in each other, forgetting the outside world for now.

CHAPTER THIRTY-SEVEN

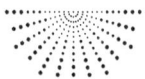

*D*arius heard the dogs barking and came back in around the side gate. He'd been gone for quite a few hours, while he'd popped home to make some phone calls for his new legitimate work, but decided he ought to check on Olivia.

Perhaps it hadn't been a good idea to invite Gabe round and then leave them to it. Olivia could be pretty feisty. She'd not spoken face to face to any of them for weeks and was still making Connie pay for setting her up, although they were finally talking again now and had even met for coffee without him. He was desperate to know what they had talked about, but Olivia wouldn't give much away. At least they hadn't killed each other, so far.

He'd made both of the women in his life a promise to stop his old job and Olivia was running intervention whenever his fingers itched to get back to the keyboard, which was often. He thought about what she'd said about his mum and knew she was right. However much it hurt, it was about time he stopped trying to impress Joan and get on with his own life. It was liberating.

He still loved Libby, but he could see that they weren't right for each other, or he could see why she thought that way at least. She would always try to conform and he needed to break free and be himself. Connie saw that and encouraged him to try new things. They had spoken about going into business together and she was excited to introduce him to her parents. Apparently, they were shocked about Greg, but open to meeting Darius, which was a good start. He had a funny feeling that Greg was still lurking around the company her dad owned, but he didn't care as long as the divorce went through.

Whistling to the dogs and seeing Olivia walk into the kitchen, her hair clean of paint and glistening and a big smile on her face, he was surprised to see Gabe still there. He was wearing a pair of damp jeans and one of the t-shirts Darius had stored in the spare room for when he stayed round. Darius raised his eyebrows at Olivia who ignored him. Gabe looked up when Darius came into the kitchen and the two men faced each other. Olivia stared between them uneasily, and then one of the dogs came running in and slid straight across the floor, bumping into Darius's legs and nearly knocking him flying. It made them all laugh and the ice was broken. Gabe moved forward from his seat on the couch and scratched Belle behind the ears. Bertie stood beside Darius and licked his hand, looking lovingly up for a cuddle.

~

*O*livia contemplated her family of people and animals who didn't quite fit in anywhere else, and rolled her eyes when Connie stuck her head around the door saying Darius had left the side gate open.

'Right, you lot,' said Olivia, with a theatrical sigh. 'Let's take the dogs for a stroll over to Winston's Café and get a late lunch for everyone. Well behaved dogs are allowed to sit beside the new tables he's put outside,' she looked pointedly at Bertie, who sat there gazing innocently at her.

Gabe got up and started looking around for the dogs' leads, which Darius strolled over and retrieved from a drawer in the utility room with a triumphant smile. Connie took the leads from him and snapped them in place on their collars. Olivia didn't comment that she looked like she'd done that before, even though she was sorely tempted.

Shutting the door behind them and taking Gabe's proffered hand, Olivia stuck her tongue out at Darius, who had just pulled Connie along by the arm to keep up with them.

'So, you two reprobates,' she called to them. 'Tell the policeman and the security expert about the new business you're setting up. Are you going into direct competition with your parents' company and Gorgeous Greg?'

'Plus, how are you going to stave off hackers?' joked Gabe, while Olivia gave him a dig in the ribs and they all laughed good-naturedly.

'On a serious note,' said Olivia. 'Do you think Winston has made any of his famous chilli that we can take home for later?'

Connie cringed at that memory and Darius kissed her lips. 'Let's just make sure that the dogs don't eat it, or they'll be dancing around all night for a different reason than those daft tutus Connie used to make you use.'

Olivia grinned and her eyes met Connie's, who flushed but smiled as Darius slid his hand around her waist making her giggle and squirm. The sun rose up from behind the pretty row of houses that Olivia used to live in and a little family with a small dog came rushing out of the flat and waved at Mr Benson, who actually waved back before he caught sight of Olivia and her friends and stomped back inside.

Winston had seen them coming and held the door open for Olivia to come inside and order, raising an eyebrow at the two sets of interlinked hands and then shrugging and going to get them coffee and a bowl of water for the dogs as they settled themselves outside. Darius and Olivia sat opposite each other and waited for the moment that Gabe sipped his coffee and then winced at the bitter taste, laughing at his expression.

The family from the flat walked past and the little boy rushed up and peered through the steamed-up window, waving at Winston, who smiled and waved back. The boy caught sight of the four friends drinking coffee outside, with the two huge dogs by their feet. He squealed and pointed at Bertie and Belle and began hopping from foot to foot, but his mother shushed him and pulled him gently away. He wouldn't give up, though, and ran back for one more look, visibly pleading with his mum to listen and to let him see the famous dancing dog. Olivia grinned with relief that she'd deleted any trace of the underwear videos when she'd started working with big brands. She picked up Bertie's paw to give him a wave, as the boy's mother caught his hand once more and, shaking her head in confusion, drew him away.

ABOUT THE AUTHOR

International bestselling author and award-winning inventor, Lizzie Chantree, started her own business at the age of 18 and became one of Fair Play London and The Patent Office's British Female Inventors of the Year in 2000. She discovered her love of writing fiction when her children were little and now works as a business mentor and runs a popular networking hour on social media, where creatives can support to each other. She writes books full of friendship and laughter, that are about women with unusual and adventurous businesses, who are far stronger than they realise. She lives with her family on the coast in Essex. Visit her website at www.lizziechantree.com or follow her on Twitter @Lizzie_Chantree

For more books and updates:
www.lizziechantree.com

I really hope you enjoyed reading The Woman Who Felt Invisible. If you liked reading my novel, please consider leaving a review. Many readers look to the reviews first when deciding which book to choose, and seeing your review might help them discover this one. I appreciate your help and support. Make an author smile today. Leave a review! Thank you so much. From Lizzie :)

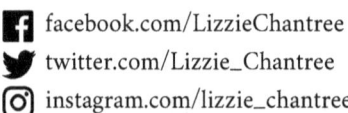

facebook.com/LizzieChantree

twitter.com/Lizzie_Chantree

instagram.com/lizzie_chantree

PRAISE FOR LIZZIE CHANTREE

'Books like this are the reason I love reading.'

'Rarely has a book held my heart in its hands the way If You Love Me I'm Yours has. An incredibly uplifting romantic story that has had me laughing and crying over and over again.'

'As always the main characters fizz and entrance, with underdogs and divas, harassed hunks and devilishly attractive but flawed rogues... The espionage aspect helps the seemingly workaday schoolyard environment along famously with catty cliques and beastly little brats, as well as adorable, yet still edgy kids.

If you haven't had the pleasure of reading one of Lizzie's books yet - treat yourself!'

'Loved the book! Lots of fiery, and glamorous characters, but there are some who are dealing with deeper issues. A book packed full of suspense. a riveting ending that made me want to keep reading. It's a romance novel, and it is about relationships, but it's also about the love a parent has for their child. Highly recommended.'

'I stepped outside my normal genre comfort zone of crime thrillers to read this book; it had been recommended to me and I had my eyes and heart opened. I laughed, I cried and had a precious insight into the life of people who on the surface appear, okay. I have bought another book from this author and started reading it immediately – such exceptional writing. I do not hesitate to recommend this book.'

THE LITTLE ICE CREAM SHOP BY THE SEA

Also from author, Lizzie Chantree.

CHAPTER 1

Not again! Genie Grayson wanted to scream and throw her hands in the air. Instead, she stuffed her fist in her mouth and turned away. She'd thought she had her terrible phobia under control – she was a perfectly sane twenty-two-year-old – but the last few weeks had been stressful, and this was her Achilles heel. She looked around furtively to see if anyone had noticed, but there was hardly anyone enjoying breakfast in her family's seafront restaurant.

The evil seagull had dropped a lump of cheese onto her pristine outdoor tablecloth. After flying right into the restaurant awning. It had obviously been at the beer that always ended up in the gutters after a busy night at one of the clubs further down the beach.

Genie rarely admitted to having this issue, as who in the world, other than herself of course, had a problem with cheese? No one who managed a restaurant and ice cream parlour, that was for sure. Not a responsible professional who served food all day and had to be surrounded by the awful stretchy stuff that smelt like her grandad's old socks after a day on his feet.

She knew if she recited the alphabet backwards she'd be ok. She'd had years of practice. She usually got to about W, and then her pulse slowed down and she was able to take a deep breath and move on. She looked up and saw the gull sitting on the wall above the restaurant, its piercing red eyes like lasers. She shushed it away, but it just turned its back on her.

She often wondered if she had an allergy to wild animals. She'd tried to pet one at a zoo on a school trip and got bitten, then her hand had swollen up and she'd been rushed to hospital, even though she'd been fine after a few hours. She'd avoided zoos ever since. She gave the jungle a wide berth too. It wasn't too difficult from her current location on the coast of Essex, but she wasn't taking any chances. Cheese, on the other hand, was impossible to dodge. Not only did she work in kitchens, she cooked when her dad had a day off. Luckily, their bestsellers were their huge breakfasts, and plates of fish and chips.

Genie knew that if she gave into the urge to shove the offending messy table into the road, she'd get herself into all kinds of trouble with her parents, and probably the local council. She was already on their radar for changing all the restaurant's lightbulbs to a deep shade of red one weekend, to create an ambience. She'd had a formal letter the following week suggesting she might be moonlighting as a sex worker. That was slander! She might be a bit busty, and she was down on her luck, but she was too tired to blink some days. She just plastered on a smile and worked through it. Takings really had to pick up, at the restaurant though. They needed more customers.

She had to find a way to calm down and reasonably work out a plan of action, either by talking to her mum, Milly, about their current dilemma, or by finding a boyfriend and having some hot steamy sex to take her mind off things.

While she pondered that thought, she grabbed the tablecloth by the edges with a couple of forks and shoved it behind the counter into the washing basket, quickly re-covering the table with a fresh cloth.

Genie smiled brightly at two school mums who were perusing the menu but her grin dropped as she turned towards the kitchen at the back of the little restaurant. She wondered if anyone would notice if she stood in the middle of the room and screamed. Probably not.

The mums were the only two customers, and they'd already caught her cursing in Spanish under her breath as she wiped down the tables when they'd arrived. They had looked at her in confusion. She'd picked up a 'learn to speak Spanish' course at the charity shop the week previously, in the hope that she might one day travel abroad with friends. She'd also thought it might help if they ever got a foreign customer, however unlikely that seemed. But when she'd got the disc back to the house, it was a home-made knock-off copy and the only vocabulary was swear-words. She hated being conned, so she'd resolutely learned the whole tape, which consisted of about fifty phrases that all sounded mightily dodgy. They were great for easing frustration, though, as no one else knew what she was saying. She hoped. She'd looked up a few of the words, but then been worried her parents would question why she was Google-translating so many profanities. She didn't want them to start to wonder if that council letter had been spot on.

Usually, the breathtaking panorama of sandy beaches and the endless skyline across the road were enough to lift her spirits. But today she felt she might as well go and bang her head against a wall, instead of trying yet again to reason with her parents. The family business *had* to be brought into the twenty-first century. She knew she had a temper and didn't always explain things clearly without combusting into flames, but they still treated her as if she was nine years old.

All she was asking of her parents was that they let her try out a few new business ideas and a handful of new ice-cream flavours. She didn't want to reinvent the wheel. Their business hadn't changed for decades. They still had the same chairs and tables, and even the menus, that her grandad Gus had installed. Her parents' restaurant, Graysons', offered bought-in, basic puddings, but Genie had seen massive growth in big gooey ice cream desserts presented in glass mugs or tall glasses. She didn't see why they couldn't try this. They had a prime site on the seafront, for goodness sake! She could feel her temper begin to rise again. Then she remembered – their customers. She didn't want to scare them away. She twirled round to face them again with another smile.

Her parents were worried about upsetting her grandad, who ran the ice cream bar. He only offered about six flavours these days. She had spent much of her time with him and her grandma when she was growing up. Her parents had stepped in to take over the business when her grandma had died a few years previously. Her grandad had begun wandering around the small garden at the back of the restaurant and shouting at the plants, raging at the loss of his wife. In the end, they'd explained to customers that he was an inventor seeing if upsetting plants stunted their growth. It was the only explanation they could come up with for his behaviour, which was becoming more and more erratic.

Their regulars knew about Genie's grandma and understood Gus's sorrow and anger, but occasionally a new customer would start to glance around to see if there were spaces to eat elsewhere, which meant even less income for them all. Genie missed her grandma Vera terribly, as she had always let her sit with them after school. Genie would perch on a high stool behind the ice cream counter and Vera would tempt her with her latest ice cream concoction and cuddle her, while Gus served a steady stream of customers anxious to get Vera's new flavours before they sold out.

With Genie's parents selling breakfasts and lunches, and Gus and Vera on ice cream, the restaurant had worked like a dream. Then her grandma died and Genie's parents had taken the reins, working harder than ever to cover their grief. They looked more frazzled as each year passed. Genie was used to coming home from school to the empty house they lived in, up the hill, as her parents were always working. Soon, she was roped into doing her homework at the restaurant, and then it seemed a natural progression for her to help out. She'd been doing that since she could walk anyway. She loved the restaurant and was proud of her family's heritage. She needed to spread her creative wings, though, and felt that since Vera had passed away, Gus was wilting. She wanted to keep her grandma's spirit alive, and Gus needed Genie more than her parents did right now.

She spent her weekend evenings making batches of ice cream for him to sell, though he kept telling her she should be out partying with people her own age, not keeping an old man company and trying to keep his business alive. He was bored one night and bought two whippy-type machines for simple, smooth ice cream and declared that she wouldn't need to help him anymore. It broke her heart. She could see that he was trying really hard to manage alone, but he was struggling with his memories of his beautiful wife and the happiness she'd given everyone with her smile and her amazing ice cream flavours. He just couldn't replicate them.

Genie had asked him about trying different recipes, but he'd harrumphed and told her that if she thought she knew better, then she could get on with it. And besides, he'd added that there wasn't enough business to try new ideas. He liked his whippy ice cream machines and they did sell a fair amount of cones, but there was no love in the ingredients. Vera used to sprinkle chocolate chips, lemon rind, tiny bites of apple and many other incredible ingredients into her mixes to make you feel like you were eating a mouthful of magic. Your tongue would tingle and most people came back to order more. People visited from miles around to try her latest flavours. Recently Genie had decided to try to keep the tradition going. After five generations of her family running this business, she was determined to make it shine again, in honour of her grandma.

As far as she was concerned, Gus had given her the green light. She'd always worked hard for her parents and was determined to turn their fortunes round. All the shops along the seafront were looking a bit tired these days. She felt they'd get stuck in a time warp if something didn't change.

She tried to calm herself down. She chanted a mantra in her head that she'd heard on the radio that morning. It was supposed to make you feel zen, but it soon irritated her now she couldn't get the stupid phrases out of her mind.

Her parents had often told Genie she was too bossy for her own good, but then, she'd had to be. Her schoolwork had suffered and she'd failed most of her exams, because she was always helping out at the restaurant or washing and cleaning at home while her parents were at work. Her parents had despaired, but what else could they have expected?

It was why she hadn't yet found a home of her own, even at her age. Her parents had moved into her grandparents' Georgian seafront property when Genie had been just two. The house and the business were their lives. She secretly couldn't imagine living anywhere else, but she'd never tell her mum and dad that. Her grandad had moved into the annex, which was separate from the main house. He'd recently paid a man to put a fence up between the two buildings, saying he needed more privacy. Genie suspected that he wanted to be able to hide away with his grief. She felt that she couldn't express her own sorrow, as she had to keep everyone else's spirits up. Her dad walked around looking permanently grumpy and her mum often wrung her hands, which in turn made Genie anxious. Genie did the restaurant books, so she knew that they could just about scrape by for now, but how long that would last for, she had no idea. They needed something to change – and fast.

Maintaining the house, her family and the restaurant was a full time job. Although none of the whole parade of restaurants were up to date, they were still quite busy as very few bars and eateries were allowed on each stretch of beach. They rarely came up for sale, tending to stay within a family. Everybody was friends with everyone else, but the décor in each venue was old fashioned, as far as Genie was concerned, and their clientele was getting older too.

That was fine, Genie respected older people, but a few tended to sit for hours, hogging the tables, and they didn't spend much money. She'd almost poked an elderly man's eye out once when she'd thought he might be dead and was checking he was still breathing. Thank goodness, he'd woken up with a start. As an only child, she loved it when there was a mix of ages mingling around. Her dad was an only child too, so there were no siblings to help him run the restaurant. It had fallen to Genie and her mum. But since Vera had died, it felt like the life and soul of the place had gone with her.

The school mums, who were regulars and probably their youngest customers, checked their designer watches to see how much time they could spend relaxing before rushing off to pick up various offspring. It was still only 9.30am, so she wandered over to take their order and chatted amiably, as she did with all their customers, biting back her frustration.

It was hard keeping up a cheerful face with the customers, when she knew that the restaurant's takings were down again that quarter. The quiet worry that seemed to be with her most days was starting to make itself more apparent. Even if it meant more of her mum's death stares, or her dad's rolling eyes, she was determined to turn the family's fortunes around.

CHAPTER 2

Ada stared out at the beautiful sea view in front of her, but couldn't really take anything in. Tears threatened to spill from her eyes, but she was tougher than that. She refused to feel sorry for herself.

Since her darling Ned passed away last year, she'd been determined to stay in the apartment they had bought together when they knew he was unwell. He'd wanted to come back home to the seaside town he'd been born in. Although it had meant leaving their friends and family behind, he yearned to wander along the sandy beaches and sit and watch the seagulls. He wanted to wriggle his bare toes in the sand and eat melting ice creams as the sun went down.

The months before he went were bittersweet. He had been at peace in his hometown, so she couldn't be cross with him for leaving her alone. She'd never lived here before, though, and the endless beaches and little shops and eateries dotted around were a far cry from her past life, full of inter-esting people and endless social engagements. Here she had a beautiful home, but her family lived abroad and she could not – would not – let them know how much she was still grieving, and move home. Here she felt close to Ned. She could run her fingers through the sand and picture him next to her doing the same. The joy on his face, when he'd recounted stories of his childhood in the old fishing town and told her of his summers building sandcastles on the beach and riding the waves with his friends. She remembered it so well.

They had only visited his birthplace once before. But as soon as he was diagnosed with his illness and given such a short time to live, he suddenly craved home.

To her, home was their huge house in America. Ned had been a celebrity photographer and they had moved often, but they had settled down in the States. She had adored the huge rooms with high ceilings and the warmth of the sun that eased her old bones, but here she was, in a new place, a place that wasn't really home for her.

Her sons called her almost daily, but so far, she'd refused to go back. Ned was here with her, she could feel him, even though she couldn't see his kind face anymore.

He would be telling her to get onto that plane and stay with their children, but they were busy. They had careers and families of their own. What would they want with a heartbroken old woman, wandering around their houses looking lost and frequently bursting into angry tears? They didn't need her dragging them down, when they were coping with their own grief. Ned had filled the room with his presence and people clamoured for his attention. He was one of those souls that others gravitated towards, to bask in the glow of his golden personality. She had been well used to it, though, and his gaze always found her in a crowded room.

She knew she could get through this, but she would have to do it in her own time. They would all probably demand that she visit them, or they would descend on her at Christmas, so until then, she had almost a year to compose herself and to let the outside world think she was recovering. She was an actress. She could do this. She would make damn sure that by the time her boys got here, they'd think she was coping beautifully, rebuilding her life and staying strong. She gripped the handrail of the panoramic balcony on her penthouse flat and gazed through a sheen of tears at the waves kissing the shore. She tried to feel some of the peace that Ned had found here.

Movement caught her eye on the promenade below and she recognised the young woman from one of the breakfast places along the beach. She was looking mutinous, even from this distance, stalking back and forward and muttering to herself. Her hands were bunched into fists and she was brandishing one of them at a very innocent-looking bush, before she swung a kick at a plant pot and then hopped about holding her toes. Ada couldn't help but smile. She had met the girl and her parents a few times and exchanged pleasantries, but Ned hadn't really wanted to eat out. She'd only been there alone, when the isolation had got too much for her. Perhaps she'd go there today and try and chase away her demons. If Genie – she remembered the girl's name at last – was in a bad mood, then they could be grumpy together. She might even have a little chat to the hedge as she walked past, too. It wouldn't answer back. She was pretty sure everyone in her building thought she was an eccentric recluse, so no-one would bat an eyelid to see her talking to a plant.

The little cafés and bars along the seafront were quaint and beautiful and looked as if they hadn't been touched by time, which was charming. Ada did think that they could do with a few modern touches, like softer cushions on their seats for frail bottoms like hers and maybe the odd tweak to the menus as a change from cooked breakfasts and chips. The beach was popular, though, and the street below was often bustling with people. It was just the restaurants that seemed eerily quiet. She couldn't understand why, as the prices were very low for the huge plates of food that were served. Seaside fry-ups were usually a crowd pleaser. They were too heavy for a little woman like her, though. She wished they offered something a bit healthier. Perhaps she ought to ask for a children's portion, but she always felt embarrassed to do that and ended up leaving at least half her meal.

Maybe if she went for brisk walks along the shoreline, then her appetite would return. She knew she was wasting away here. Her children would be horrified if they could see how much weight she'd lost. She always hid most of her body behind a table when they video-chatted with her. She wore a bulky jumper and stuck a smile on her face and told them she was *fine*.

She straightened her back, which ached slightly from all her tossing and turning at night. She often thought she must be searching for Ned in her sleep, as she woke up feeling like she'd done a workout. She felt the worse for it, not better. Her building had a gym downstairs and a spa, but she'd never ventured in. She used to swim every day at her old home, but now she worried that she'd pass out through exhaustion while in the pool, and hadn't plucked up the courage to risk it yet.

She occasionally wondered if she should just let herself drift off and be with Ned, but she was stronger than that. She would survive this. Brushing a tear from her eye, she turned and decided that she needed some fresh air. In fact, today was going to be the day when that huge breakfast at Genie's restaurant didn't defeat her.

CHAPTER 3

Genie smiled politely at the little woman in front of her, who was becoming a regular. She had beautiful skin, and her soft grey hair was always pulled back into a perfect chignon, but her eyes were so sad. Genie didn't know her well enough to ask her if she was ok, but she could feel the unhappiness emanating from her, even though she always looked up at her with a bright smile.

Today she was working her way through a huge plate of food and had been bravely tackling it for the last hour. She had only got about a third of the way through, and looked exhausted. Genie had once asked her parents to offer smaller portions for different sized appetites, but they had told her not to be silly, their prices were so cheap and no one would want a smaller plate for the same money. Genie secretly thought they overloaded the plates too much. If they would just take two or three ingredients off the breakfasts and add them as extras, they would make much more money. People could still have a hearty breakfast, but the pound or two on each plate for beans, mushrooms, and extra toast would make such a difference to their bottom line. It would give them a chance to improve everything else.

Genie took Ada the fresh pot of tea she'd asked for and gave her a warm smile. There was something about her that drew Genie to her. She wanted to reach out and give her a supportive hug. Instead, she whipped the plate away as soon as the lady put her cutlery down and was rewarded with a grateful glance. A woman that size probably ate muesli for breakfast, lunch and dinner.

Genie looked down at her own ample hips and bulging bosom and decided that she was going to try and take her nextdoor neighbour's dog out for a morning walk along the shore more often. She'd also try not feel so stressed that she couldn't be bothered to cook a proper meal at night. Her parents loved food that was quick and easy to whip up, but Genie enjoyed fresh ingredients and spent ages scanning new recipe ideas and trying out different flavours at home. It didn't have to take an age to make a meal from scratch – as long as it didn't contain cheese. If it did, she had to put on gloves to handle it. This often caused her to spill most of the ingredients. She'd then have to put on wellington boots to sweep up the disgusting, cheesy tendrils before they touched her toes. Genie's parents had lost a bit of weight recently, but this might have been because they were stressed out about the businesses along the seafront, rather than her delicious evening meals.

She eyed her dad's not-quite-so portly stomach. She was pleased to see he was in slightly better shape these days. He wasn't as grumpy either. Her mum, on the other hand, always made an effort with her appearance and scolded Genie about being such a slob. But Genie didn't have time to spend ages shopping with friends for the latest fashions. Besides, her clothes usually stank of grease from the fryer in the back kitchen by the time she got home, so she had given up on that years ago. She was clean and presentable at work, with her long dark hair pulled back in a ponytail to keep it away from the food (and cheese) and a fresh blouse and skirt every day. Even that seemed an effort.

She had piercing blue eyes that customers often stopped her to ask about, and long silky black lashes, which meant she didn't need much make-up. Her skin was slightly tanned from working outdoors, even at this time of year. Half the chairs and tables were inside, but the other half were under an awning. This could be swept back at the touch of a button, allowing diners to sit in the sunshine. The British weather was actually good this year, so the awning was open for a lot of the time, even though Christmas wasn't all that long ago.

Genie glanced up from a table she was clearing. Trudie, from one of the other restaurants further along, had popped her head in to say hello. She glanced around to see if they were busy and grinned a hello at Genie.

'Hey Trudie, how's business today?'

Trudie paused to say hello to Ada, which surprised Genie, as she'd thought the older lady pretty much kept herself to herself. Ada greeted her politely and then turned back to her tea.

'We're really busy,' said Trudie. 'And I've run out of milk already. I forgot to send the order today. We've got a coach party in and they're causing havoc, moving all the tables round.' Trudie smiled happily.

Genie knew she wouldn't mind a huge crowd. These businesses were used to being packed to the rafters at weekends, but being busy on a weekday and not having to pace up and down the road looking for customers was a complete bonus.

Genie grinned at the other woman's infectious smile. Everyone along the parade called her Tantalising Trudie, because her hips swayed mesmerizingly as she weaved between tables. Trudie kept Genie sane and was always dropping in for a chat with her or her parents. Genie had tried to copy Trudie's sashay once and had tripped over and almost landed face-first in the lap of one of their male customers. She'd looked up to apologise, and seen Bob from the local council office staring disapprovingly down at her, his face bright red. She wouldn't be trying that move again in a hurry.

Everyone along this parade of restaurants got on so well. It was what had kept Genie going when her own friends stopped coming to the restaurant and she had fewer people of her own age to chat to. Trudie was more her mother's friend than hers, but they still got on really well.

'Of course!' she responded to Trudie's appeal for milk. 'I'm sure Dad ordered enough and we're quiet today, so I'll grab you a couple of cartons.'

Trudie smiled her thanks and pulled out a chair and sat chatting quietly to Ada, who seemed pleased at the interruption. When Genie returned, Trudie jumped up, waved her thanks and jogged back to her own establishment, waving to Genie's dad who had just come out of the kitchen with huge breakfasts for a table of two.

ALSO BY LIZZIE CHANTREE

Romantic Fiction

The Cherry Blossom Lane Series

Book 1

My Perfect Ex

Book 2

The One That He Wants

Book 3

The Eternal Bachelor

The Little Shop By The Sea Series

Book 1

The Little Ice Cream Shop By The Sea

Book 2

The Little Cupcake Shop By The Sea

If You Love Me, I'm Yours

The Woman Who Felt Invisible

Ninja School Mum

Babe Driven

Love's Child

Finding Gina

Shh... It's Our Secret

Non-Fiction

<u>Networking For Writers</u>